The Loudwater Mystery

By Edgar Jepson

Originally published in 1920

The Loudwater Mystery

© 2010 Resurrected Press
www.ResurrectedPress.com

Published by Intrepid Ink, LLC

Intrepid Ink, LLC provides full publishing services to authors of fiction and non-fiction books, eBooks and websites. From editing to formatting, to publishing, to marketing, Intrepid Ink gets your creative works into the hands of the people who want to read them.
Find out more at www.IntrepidInk.com.

ISBN 13: 978-1-935774-27-3

Printed in the United States of America

FOREWORD

The Loudwater Mystery was published at the beginning of what has been termed the "Golden Age" of British mysteries; that period between the two world wars which marked the heyday of the form. This was the period that saw the first works of Agatha Christie and Dorothy Sayers, when the goal of the mystery writer was to present a clever puzzle which the detective had to solve, often presenting the solution in a climactic drawing room scene.

The Loudwater Mystery may lack such a final scene, but it contains most of the other elements of a classic "Golden Age" mystery. First, there is the locale, the Loudwater estate, with the suspects all coming from the immediate neighborhood. Second, there is the abundance of suspects with suspicions falling on each by turn. Third, there is the crime itself, the murder of Lord Loudwater, who it seems, no one will really miss. Finally, there is the obligatory detective, Flexen, who must make sense of the situation, a task made more difficult by the fact that everyone is lying on some point or other relating to the crime. Flexen is no Poirot or Peter Wimsey, but he is a good judge of when he is being lied to and he is nothing if not persistent.

The story follows the classic format, with contradictory evidence given by each of the suspects. At least five people were known to have been present at the scene of the crime, but with Flexen unable to establish even the time of death, deducing the culprit proves difficult. All this is further complicated by three separate romances taking place in the background.

All in all, Jepson has provided in *The Loudwater Mystery* a witty and entertaining tale of crime and detection.

About the Author

Edgar Alfred Jepson (1863-1938) was an English writer of adventure and detective fiction. He also wrote supernatural and fantasy stories. In addition to writing, he translated a number of works including the Arsene Lupin stories of Maurice Leblanc. Both a son and a daughter were successful writers, as is a granddaughter.

Greg Fowlkes
Editor-In-Chief
Resurrected Press
www.ResurrectedPress.com

1

Lord Loudwater was paying attention neither to his breakfast nor to the cat Melchisidec. Absorbed in a leader in *The Times* newspaper, now and again he tugged at his red-brown beard in order to quicken his comprehension of the weighty phrases of the leader-writer; now and again he made noises, chiefly with his nose, expressive of disgust. Lady Loudwater paid no attention to these noises. She did not even raise her eyes to her husband's face. She ate her breakfast with a thoughtful air, her brow puckered by a faint frown.

She also paid no attention to her favourite, Melchisidec. Melchisidec, unduly excited by the smell of grilled sole, came to Lord Loudwater, rose on his hind legs, laid his paws on his trousers, and stuck some claws into his thigh. It was no more than gentle, arresting pricks; but the tender nobleman sprang from his chair with a short howl, kicked with futile violence a portion of the empty air which Melchisidec had just vacated, staggered, and nearly fell.

Lady Loudwater did not laugh; but she did cough.

Her husband, his face a furious crimson, glared at her with reddish eyes, and swore violently at her and the cat.

Lady Loudwater rose, her face flushed, her lips trembling, picked up Melchisidec, and walked out of the room. Lord Loudwater scowled at the closed door, sat down, and went on with his breakfast.

James Hutchings, the butler, came quietly into the room, took one of the smaller dishes from the sideboard and Lady Loudwater's teapot from the table. He went quietly out of the room, pausing at the door to scowl at his master's back. Lady Loudwater finished her breakfast in the sitting-room of her suite of rooms on the first floor. She was no longer inattentive to Melchisidec.

During her breakfast she put all consideration of her husband's behaviour out of her mind. As she smoked a cigarette after breakfast she considered it for a little while. She often had to consider it. She came to the conclusion to which she had often come before: that she owed him nothing whatever. She came to the further conclusion that she detested him. She had far too good a brow not to be able to see a fact clearly. She wished more heartily than ever that she had never married him. It had been a grievous mistake; and it seemed likely to last a life-time—her life-time. The last five ancestors of her husband had lived to be eighty. His father would doubtless have lived to be eighty too, had he not broken his neck in the hunting-field at the age of fifty-four. On the other hand, none of the Quaintons, her own family, had reached the age of sixty. Lord Loudwater was thirty-five; she was twenty-two; he would therefore survive her by at least seven years. She would certainly be bowed down all her life under this grievous burden.

It was an odd calculation for a young married woman to make; but Lady Loudwater came of an uncommon family, which had produced more brilliant, irresponsible, and passably unscrupulous men than any other of the leading families in England. Her father had been one of them. She took after him. Moreover, Lord Loudwater would have induced odd reveries in any wife. He had been intolerable since the second week of their honeymoon. Wholly without power of self-restraint, the furious outbursts of his vile temper had been consistently revolting. She once more told herself that something would have to be done about it—not on the instant, however. At the moment there appeared to her to be months to do it in. She dropped her cigarette end into the ash-tray, and with it any further consideration of the manners and disposition of Lord Loudwater.

She lit another cigarette and let her thoughts turn to that far more appealing subject, Colonel Antony Grey. They turned to him readily and wholly. In less than three minutes she was seeing his face and hearing certain tones in his voice with amazing clearness. Once she looked at the clock impatiently. It was half-past ten. She would not see him till three—four and a half hours. It seemed a long while to her. However, she could go on thinking about him. She did.

While she considered her ill-tempered husband her eyes had been hard and almost shallow. While she considered Colonel Grey, they grew soft and deep. Her lips had been set and almost thin; now they grew most kissable.

Lord Loudwater finished his breakfast, the scowl on his face fading slowly to a frown. He lit a cigar and with a moody air went to his smoking-room. The criminal carelessness of the cat Melchisidec still rankled.

As he entered the room, half office and half smoking-room, Mr. Herbert Manley, his secretary, bade him good morning. Lord Loudwater returned his greeting with a scowl.

Mr. Herbert Manley had one of those faces which begin well and end badly. He had a fine forehead, lofty and broad, a well-cut, gently-curving-nose, a slack, thick-lipped mouth, always a little open, a heavy, animal jaw, and the chin of an eagle. His fine, black hair was thin on the temples. His moustache was thin and straggled. His black eyes were as good as his brow, intelligent, observant, and alert. It was plain that had his lips been thinner and his chin larger he would not have been the secretary of Lord Loudwater—or of anyone else. He would have been a masterless man.

The success of two one-act plays on the stage of the
music-halls had given him the firm hope of one day
becoming a masterless man as a successful dramatist.
His post gave him the leisure to write plays. But for the
fact that it brought him into such frequent contact with
the Lord Loudwater it would have been a really pleasant
post: the food was excellent; the wine was good; the
library was passable; and the servants, with the
exception of James Hutchings, liked and respected him.
He had the art of making himself valued (at far more
than his real worth, said his enemies), and his air of
importance continuously impressed them.

With a patient air he began to discuss the morning's
letters, and ask for instructions. Lord Loudwater was, as
often happened, uncommonly captious about the letters.
He had not recovered from the shock the inconsiderate
Melchisidec had given his nerves. The instructions he
gave were somewhat muddled; and when Mr. Manley
tried to get them clearer, his employer swore at him for
an idiot. Mr. Manley persisted firmly through much
abuse till he did get them clear. He had come to consider
his employer's furies an unfortunate weakness which had
to be endured by the holder of the post he found so
advantageous. He endured them with what stoicism he
might.

Lord Loudwater in a bad temper always produced a
strong impression of redness for a man whose colouring
was merely red-brown. Owing to the fact that his fierce,
protruding blue eyes were red-rimmed and somewhat
bloodshot, in moments of emotion they shone with a
curious red glint, and his florid face flushed a deeper red.
In these moments Mr. Manley had a feeling that he was
dealing with a bad-tempered red bull. His employer made
very much the same impression on other people, but few
of them had the impression of bullness so clear and so
complete as did Mr. Manley. Lady Loudwater, on the
other hand, felt always, whether her husband was

ramping or quiet, that she was dealing with a bad-tempered bull.

Presently they came to the end of the letters. Lord Loudwater lit another cigar, and scowled thoughtfully. Mr. Manley gazed at his scowling face and wondered idly whether he would ever light on another human being whom he would detest so heartily as he detested his employer. He thought it indeed unlikely. Still, when he became a successful dramatist there might be an actor-manager—

Then Lord Loudwater said: "Did you tell Mrs. Truslove that after September her allowance would be reduced to three hundred a year?"

"Yes," said Mr. Manley.

"What did she say?"

Mr. Manley hesitated; then he said diplomatically: "She did not seem to like it."

"What did she *say*?" cried Lord Loudwater in a sudden, startling bellow, and his eyes shone red.

Mr. Manley winced and said quickly: "She said it was just like you."

"Just like me? Hey? And what did she mean by that?" cried Lord Loudwater loudly and angrily.

Mr. Manley expressed utter ignorance by looking blank and shrugging his shoulders.

"The jade! She's had six hundred a year for more than two years. Did she think it would go on forever?" cried his employer.

"No," said Mr. Manley.

"And why didn't she think it would go on forever? Hey?" said Lord Loudwater in a challenging tone.

"Because there wasn't an actual deed of settlement," said Mr. Manley.

"The ungrateful jade! I've a good mind to stop it altogether!" cried his employer.

Mr. Manley said nothing. His face was blank; it neither approved nor disapproved the suggestion.

Lord Loudwater scowled at him and said: "I expect she said she wished she'd never had anything to do with me."

"No," said Mr. Manley.

"I'll bet that's what she thinks," growled Lord Loudwater.

Mr. Manley let the suggestion pass without comment. His face was blank.

"And what's she going to do about it?" said Lord Loudwater in a tone of challenge.

"She's going to see you about it."

"I'm damned if she is!" cried Lord Loudwater hastily, in a much less assured tone.

Mr. Manley permitted a faint, sceptical smile to wreathe his lips.

"What are you grinning at? If you think she'll gain anything by doing that, she won't," said Lord Loudwater, with a blustering truculence.

Mr. Manley wondered. Helena Truslove was a lady of considerable force of character. He suspected that if Lord Loudwater had ever been afraid of a fellow-creature, he must at times have been afraid of Helena Truslove. He fancied that now he was not nearly as fearless as he sounded. He did not say so.

His employer was silent, buried in scowling reflection. Mr. Manley gazed at him without any great intentness, and came to the conclusion that he did not merely detest him, he loathed him.

Presently he said: "There's a cheque from Hanbury and Johnson for twelve thousand and forty-six pounds for the rubber shares your lordship sold. It wants endorsing."

He handed the cheque across the table to Lord Loudwater. Lord Loudwater dipped his pen in the ink, transfixed a struggling bluebottle, and drew it out.

"Why the devil don't you see that the ink is fresh?" he roared.

"It is fresh. The bluebottle must have just fallen into it," said Mr. Manley in an unruffled tone.

Lord Loudwater cursed the bluebottle, restored it to the ink-pot, endorsed the cheque, and tossed it across the table to Mr. Manley.

"By the way," said Mr. Manley, with some hesitation, "there's another anonymous letter."

"Why didn't you burn it? I told you to burn 'em all," snapped his employer.

"This one is not about you. It's about Hutchings," said Mr. Manley in an explanatory tone.

"Hutchings? What about Hutchings?"

"You'd better read it," said Mr. Manley, handing him the letter. "It seems to be from some spiteful woman."

The letter was indeed written in female handwriting, and it accused the butler, wordily enough, of having received a commission from Lord Loudwater's wine merchants on a purchase of fifty dozen of champagne which he had bought from them a month before. It further stated that he had received a like commission on many other such purchases.

Lord Loudwater read it, scowling, sprang up from his chair with his eyes protruding further than usual, and cried: "The scoundrel! The blackguard! I'll teach him! I'll gaol him!"

He dashed at the electric bell by the fireplace, set his thumb on it, and kept it there.

Holloway, the second footman, came running. The servants knew their master's ring. They always ran to answer it, after some discussion as to which of them should go.

He entered and said: "Yes, m'lord?"

"Send that scoundrel Hutchings to me! Send him at once!" roared his master.

"Yes, m'lord," said Holloway, and hurried away.

He found James Hutchings in his pantry, told him that their master wanted him, and added that he was in a tearing rage.

Hutchings, who never expected his sanguine and irascible master to be in any other mood, finished the paragraph of the article in the *Daily Telegraph* he was reading, put on his coat, and went to the study. His delay gave Lord Loudwater's wrath full time to mature.

When the butler entered his master shook his fist at him and roared: "You scoundrel! You infernal scoundrel! You've been robbing me! You've been robbing me for years, you blackguard!"

James Hutchings met the charge with complete calm. He shook his head and said in a surly tone: "No; I haven't done anything of the kind, m'lord."

The flat denial infuriated his master yet more. He spluttered and was for a while incoherent. Then he became again articulate and said: "You have, you rogue! You took a commission–a secret commission on that fifty dozen of champagne I bought last month. You've been doing it for years."

James Hutchings' surly face was transformed. It grew malignant; his fierce, protruding, red-rimmed blue eyes sparkled balefully, and he flushed to a redness as deep as that of his master. He knew at once who had betrayed him, and he was furious–at the betrayal. At the same time, he was not greatly alarmed; he had never received a cheque from the wine merchants; all their payments to him had been in cash, and he had always cherished a warm contempt for his master.

"I haven't," he said fiercely. "And if I had it would be quite regular–only a perquisite."

For the hundredth time Mr. Manley remarked the likeness between Lord Loudwater and his butler. They had the same fierce, protruding, red-rimmed blue eyes, the same narrow, low forehead, the same large ears. Hutchings' hair was a darker brown than Lord Loudwater's, and his lips were thinner. But Mr. Manley was sure that, had he worn a beard instead of whiskers, it would have been difficult for many people to be sure which was Lord Loudwater and which his butler.

Lord Loudwater again spluttered; then he roared: "A perquisite! What about the Corrupt Practices Act? It was passed for rogues like you! I'll show you all about perquisites! You'll find yourself in gaol inside of a month."

"I shan't. There isn't a word of truth in it, or a scrap of evidence," said Hutchings fiercely.

"Evidence? I'll find evidence all right!" cried his master. "And if I don't, I'll, anyhow, discharge you without a character. I'll get you one way or another, my fine fellow! I'll teach you to rob me!"

"I haven't robbed your lordship," said Hutchings in a less surly tone.

He was much more moved by the threat of discharge than the threat of prosecution.

"I tell you you have. And you can clear out of this. I'll wire to town at once for another butler—an honest butler. You'll clear out the moment he comes. Pack up and be ready to go. And when you do go, I'll give you twenty-four hours to clear out of the country before I put the police on your track," cried Lord Loudwater.

Mr. Manley observed that it was exactly like him to take no risk, in spite of his fury, of any loss of comfort from the lack of a butler. The instinct of self-protection was indeed strong in him.

"Not a bit of it. You've told me to go, and I'm going at once—this very day. The police will find me at my father's for the next fortnight," said Hutchings with a sneer. "And when I go to London I'll leave my address."

"A lot of good your going to London will do you. I'll see you never get another place in this country," snarled Lord Loudwater.

Hutchings gave him a look of vindictive malignity so intense that it made Mr. Manley quite uncomfortable, turned, and went out of the room.

Lord Loudwater said: "I'll teach the scoundrel to rob me! Write at once for a new butler."

He took some lumps of sugar from a jar on the mantelpiece, and went through the door which opened into the library.

In the library he stopped and shouted back: "If Morton comes about the timber, I shall be in the stables."

Then he went through one of the long windows of the library into the garden and took his way to the stables. As he drew near them the scowl cleared from his face. But it remained a formidable face; it did not grow pleasant. None the less, he spent a pleasant hour in the stables, petting his horses. He was fond of horses, not of cats, and he never bullied and seldom abused his horses as he abused and bullied his fellow men and women. This was the result of his experience. He had learnt from it that he might bully and abuse his human dependents with impunity. As a boy he had also bullied and abused his horses. But in his eighteenth year he had been savaged by a young horse he had maltreated, and the lesson had stuck in his mind. It was a simple, obtuse mind, but it had formed the theory that he got more out of human beings, more deference and service, by bullying them and more out of horses by treating them kindly. Besides, he liked horses.

Mr. Manley did not set about answering the letters at once. He reflected for a while on the likeness between Hutchings and his master. He thought the physical likeness of little interest. There was a whole clan of Hutchingses in the villages and woods round the castle, the bulk of them gamekeepers; and there had been for generations. Mr. Manley was much more interested in the resemblance in character between Hutchings and Lord Loudwater. Hutchings, probably under the pressure of circumstances, was much less of a bore than his master, but quite as much of a bully. Also, he was more intelligent, and consequently more dangerous. Mr. Manley would on no account have had him look at him with the intense malignity with which he had looked at his master. Doubtless the butler had far greater self-control than Lord Loudwater; but if ever he did lose it it would be uncommonly bad for Lord Loudwater.

It would be interesting to find in the Loudwater archives the common ancestor to whom they both cast so directly back. He fancied that it must be the third Baron. At any rate, both had his protruding blue eyes, softened in his portrait doubtless by the natural politeness of the fashionable painter. Was it worth his while to look up the record of the third Lord Loudwater? He decided that, if he found himself at sufficient leisure, he would. Then he decided that he was glad that Hutchins was going; the butler had shown him but little civility. Then he set about answering the letters.

When he had finished them he took up the stockbroker's cheque and considered it with a thoughtful frown. He had never before seen a cheque for so large a sum; and it interested him. Then he wrote a short note of instructions to Lord Loudwater's bankers. The ink in his fountain-pen ran out as he came to the end of it, and he signed it with the pen with which Lord Loudwater had endorsed the cheque. He put the cheque into the envelope he had already addressed, put stamps on all the letters, carried them to the post-box on a table in the hall, went through the library out into the garden, and smoked a cigarette with a somewhat languid air. Then he went into the library and took up his task of cataloguing the books at the point at which he had stopped the day before. He often paused to dip at length into a book before entering it in the catalogue. He did not believe in hasty work.

2

Lord Loudwater came to lunch in a better temper than that in which he had left the breakfast-table. He had ridden eight miles round and about his estate, and the ride had soothed that seat of the evil humours–his liver. Lady Loudwater had been careful to shut Melchisidec in her boudoir; James Hutchings had no desire in the world to see his master's florid face or square back, and had instructed Wilkins and Holloway, the first and second footmen, to wait at table. Lord Loudwater therefore could, without any ruffling of his sensibilities, give all his thought to his food, and he did. The cooking at the castle was always excellent. If it was not, he sent for the chef and spoke to him about it.

There was little conversation at lunch. Lady Loudwater never spoke to her husband first, save on rare occasions about a matter of importance. It was not that she perceived any glamour of royalty about him; she did not wish to hear his voice. Besides, she had never found a conversational opening so harmless that he could not contrive, were it his whim, to be offensive about it. Besides, she had at the moment nothing to say to him.

In truth, owing to the fact that she took so many practically silent meals with him, she was becoming rather a gourmet. The food, naturally the most important fact, had become really the most important fact at the meals they took together. She had come to realize this. It was the only advantage she had ever derived from her intercourse with her husband.

At this lunch, however, she did not pay as much attention to the food as usual, not indeed as much as it deserved. Her mind would stray from it to Colonel Grey.

She wondered what he would tell her about herself that afternoon. He was always discovering possibilities in her which she had never discovered for herself. She only perceived their existence when he pointed them out to her. Then they became obvious. Also, he was always discovering fresh facts, attractive facts, about her–about her eyes and lips and hair and figure. He imparted each discovery to her as he made it, without delay, and with the genuine enthusiasm of a discoverer. Of course, he should not have done this. It was, indeed, wrong. But he had assured her that he could not help it, that he was always blurting things out. Since it was a habit of long standing, now probably ingrained, it was useless to reproach him with any great severity for his frankness. She did not do so.

For his part, the Lord Loudwater had but little to say to his wife. She was fond of Melchisidec and indifferent to horses. For the greater part of the meal he was hardly aware that she was at the other end of the table. Immersed in his food and its deglutition, he was hardly sensible of the outside world at all. Once, disturbed by Holloway's removing his empty plate, he told her that he had seen a dog-fox on Windy Ridge; again, when Holloway handed the cheese-straws to him, he told her that Merry Belle's black colt had a cold. Her two replies, "Oh, did you?" and "Has he?" appeared to fall on deaf ears. He did not continue either conversation.

Then Lord Loudwater broke into an eloquent monologue. Wilkins had poured out a glass of port for both of them to drink with their cheese-straws. Lord Loudwater finished his cheese-straws, took a long sip from his glass, rolled it lovingly over his tongue, gulped it down with a hideous grimace, banged down his fist on the table, and roared in a terrible, anguished voice:

"It's corked! It's corked! It's that scoundrel Hutchings! This is his way of taking it out of me for sacking him. He's done it on purpose, the scoundrel! Now I will gaol him! Hanged if I don't!"

"I'll get another bottle, m'lord," said Wilkins, catching up the decanter, and hurrying towards the door.

"Get it! And be quick about it! And tell that scoundrel I'll gaol him!" cried Lord Loudwater.

Wilkins rushed from the room bearing in his hand the decanter of offending port; Holloway followed him to help.

Lady Loudwater sipped a little port from her glass. She was rather inclined to take no one's word for anything which she could herself verify. Then she took another sip.

Then she said; "Are you sure this wine's corked?"

Corked wine at the end of a really good meal is a bitter blow to any man, an exceedingly bitter blow to a man of Lord Loudwater's sensitiveness in such matters.

"Am I sure? Hey? Am I sure? Yes! I am sure, you little fool!" he bellowed. "What do you know about wine? Talk about things you understand!"

Lady Loudwater's face was twisted by a faint spasm of hate which left it flushed. She would never grow used to being bellowed at for a fool. Once more her husband's refusal to let her take her meals apart from him seemed monstrous. Hardly ever did she rise from one at which she had not been abused and insulted. She realized indeed that she had been foolish to ask the question. But why should she sit tongue-tied before the brute?

She took another sip and said quietly: "It isn't corked."

Then she turned cold with fright.

Lord Loudwater could not believe his ears. It could not be that his wife had contradicted him flatly. It–could–*not*–be.

He was still incredulous, breathing heavily, when the door opened and James Hutchings appeared on the threshold. In his right hand he held the decanter of offending port, in his left a sound cork.

He said firmly: "This wine isn't corked, m'lord. Its flavour is perfect. Besides, a cork like this couldn't cork it."

A less sensitive man than Lord Loudwater might have risen to the double emergency. Lord Loudwater could not. He sat perfectly still. But his eyes rolled so horribly that the Lady Loudwater started from her chair, uttered a faint scream, and fairly ran through the long window into the garden.

James Hutchings advanced to the table, thumped the decanter down on it–no way to treat an old vintage port– at Lord Loudwater's right hand, walked out of the room, and shut the door firmly behind him.

In the great hall he smiled a triumphant, malevolent smile. Then he called Wilkins and Holloway, who stood together in the middle of it, cowardly dogs and shirkers, and strode past them to the door to the servants' quarters.

A few moments later Lord Loudwater rose to his feet and staggered dizzily along to the other end of the table. He picked up his wife's half-emptied glass and sipped the port. It was *not* corked. It was incredible! He would never forgive her!

He rang the bell. Both Wilkins and Holloway answered it. He bade them tell Hutchings to pack his belongings and go at once. If he were not out of the castle by four o'clock, they were to kick him out. Then he went, still scowling, to the stables.

Mr. Manley had already finished his lunch. Halfway through his after-lunch pipe he rose, took his hat and stick, and set out to pay a visit to Mrs. Truslove.

As he came out of the park gates he came upon the Rev. George Stebbing, the *locum tenens* in charge of the parish, for the vicar was away on a holiday, enjoying a respite from his perpetual struggle with the patron of the living, Lord Loudwater.

They fell into step and for a while discussed the local weather and local affairs. Then Mr. Manley, who had been gifted by Heaven with a lively imagination wholly untrammelled by any straining passion for exactitude, entertained Mr. Stebbing with a vivid account of his experiences as leader of the first Great Push. Mr. Manley was one of the many rather stout, soft men who in different parts of Great Britain will till their dying days entertain acquaintances with vivid accounts of their experiences as leaders of the Great Pushes. Like that of most of them, his war experience, before his weak heart had procured him his discharge from the army, had consisted wholly of office work in England. His account of his strenuous fighting lacked nothing of fire or picturesqueness on that account. He was too modest to say in so many words that but for his martial qualities there would have been no Great Push at all, and that any success it had had was due to those martial qualities, but that was the impression he left on Mr. Stebbing's simple and rather plastic mind. When therefore they parted at the crossroads, Mr. Manley went on his way in a pleasant content at having once more made himself valued; and Mr. Stebbing went on his way feeling thankful that he had been brought into friendly contact with a really able hero. Both of them were the happier for their chance meeting.

Mr. Manley found Helena Truslove in her drawing-room, and when the door closed behind the maid who had ushered him into it, he embraced her with affectionate warmth. Then he held her out at arm's-length, and for the several hundredth time admired her handsome, clear-skinned, high-coloured, gipsy face, her black, rather wild eyes, and the black hair wreathed round her head in so heavy a mass.

"It has been an awful long time between the kisses," he said.

She sighed a sigh of content and laughed softly. Then she said: "I sometimes think that you must have had a great deal of practice."

"No," said Mr. Manley firmly. "I have never had occasion to be in love before."

He put her back into the chair from which he had lifted her, sat down facing her, and gazed at her with adoring eyes. He was truly very much in love with her.

They were excellent complements the one of the other. If Mr. Manley had the brains for two—indeed, he had the brains for half a dozen—she had the character for two. Her chin was very unlike the chin of an eagle. She was not, indeed, lacking in brains. Her brow forbade the supposition. But hers was rather the practical intelligence, his the creative. That she had the force of character, on occasion the fierceness, which he lacked, was no small source of her attraction for him.

"And how was the hog this morning?" she said, ready to be soothing.

"The hog" was their pet name for Lord Loudwater.

"Beastly. He's an utterly loathsome fellow," said Mr. Manley with conviction.

"Oh, no; not utterly—at any rate, not if you're independent of him," she protested.

"Does he ever come into contact with anyone who is not dependent on him? I believe he shuns them like the pest."

"Not into close contact," she said—"at any rate, nowadays. But I've known him to do good-natured things; and then he's very fond of his horses."

"That makes the way he treats every human being who is in any way dependent on him all the more disgusting," said Mr. Manley firmly.

"Oh, I don't know. It's something to be fond of animals," she said tolerantly.

"This morning he had a devil of a row with Hutchings, the butler, you know, and discharged him."

"That was a silly thing to do. Hutchings is not at all a good person to have a row with," she said quickly. "I should say that he was a far more dangerous brute than

Loudwater and much more intelligent. Still, I don't know what he could do. What was the row about?"

"Some woman sent Loudwater an anonymous letter accusing Hutchings of having received commissions from the wine merchants."

"That would be Elizabeth Twitcher's mother. Elizabeth and Hutchings were engaged, and about ten days ago he jilted her," said Mrs. Truslove. "I suppose that when he was in love with her he bragged about these commissions to her and she told her mother."

"Her mother has certainly taken it out of him for jilting her daughter. But what an unsavoury place the castle is!" said Mr. Manley.

"With such a master—what can you expect?" said Mrs. Truslove. "Did the hog say anything more about halving my allowance?"

Mr. Manley frowned. A few days before he had been greatly surprised to learn from Lord Loudwater that the bulk of Helena Truslove's income was an allowance from him. The matter had greatly exercised his mind. Why should his employer allow her six hundred a year? It was a matter which should be cleared up.

He said slowly: "Yes, he did. He asked what you said when I told you that he was going to halve it, and he did not seem to like the idea of your seeing him about it."

"He'll like my seeing him about it even less than the idea of it," said Mrs. Truslove firmly, and there was a sudden gleam in her wild black eyes.

Mr. Manley looked at her, frowning faintly. Then he said in a rather hesitating manner: "I've never asked you about it. But why does the hog make you this allowance?"

"That's my dark past," she said in a teasing tone, smiling at him. "I suppose that as we're going to be married so soon I ought to make a clean breast of it, if you really want to know."

"Just as you like," said Mr. Manley, his face clearing a little at her careless tone.

"Well, the hog treated me badly—not really badly, because I didn't care enough about him to make it possible for him to treat me really badly, but just as badly as he could. For when he and I first met I was on the way to get engaged to a man, named Hardwicke—a rich city man, rather a bore, but a man who would make an excellent husband. Loudwater knew that Hardwicke was ready and eager to marry me, and I suppose that that helped to make him keen on me. At any rate, he made love to me, not nearly so badly as you'd think, and persuaded me to promise to marry him."

"I can't think how you could have done it!" cried Mr. Manley.

"How was I to know what a hog he was at home? At Trouville he was quite nice, as I tell you. Besides, there was the title—I thought I should like to be Lady Loudwater. You know, I do have strong impulses, and I act on them."

"Well, after all, you didn't marry him," said Mr. Manley in a tone of relief. "What did happen?"

"We were engaged for about two months. Then, about a month before the date fixed for our marriage, he met Olivia Quainton, fell in love with her, and broke off our engagement a week before our wedding-day."

"Well, of all the caddish tricks!" cried Mr. Manley.

"You can imagine how furious I was. And I wasn't going to stand it—not from Loudwater, at any rate. I had learnt a good deal more about him in the eleven weeks we were engaged, and, naturally, I wasn't pleased with what I had learnt. I set out to make myself very disagreeable. I saw him and did make myself very disagreeable. I told him a good many unpleasant things about himself which made him much more furious than I was myself."

"I'm glad some of it got through his thick skin," said Mr. Manley.

"A good deal of it did. Then I made it clear to him that he had robbed me of John Hardwicke and an excellent settlement in life, and told him that I was going to bring an action for breach of promise against him. That certainly got through his thick skin, for it's very painful to him to spend money on anyone but himself. But he made terms at once, gave me this house furnished, and promised to allow me six hundred a year for life. You don't think I was wrong to take it?" she added anxiously.

"Certainly not," said Mr. Manley quickly and firmly.

Her face cleared and she said: "So many people would say that it was not nice my taking money for an injury like that."

"Rubbish! It wasn't as if you'd been in love with him," said Mr. Manley with the firmest conviction.

"That's the exact point. You do see things," she said, smiling at him gratefully. "If I had been, it would have been quite different."

"And how else were you to score off him except by hitting him in the pocket? That and his stomach are his only vulnerable points," said Mr. Manley viciously.

He was ignorant of Melchisidec's discovery of another.

"They are. And he certainly had robbed me of an income. It was only fair that he should make up for it," she said rather plaintively.

"Absolutely fair."

"Well, those were the terms. The house is mine all right; it was properly made over to me. But, stupidly, I didn't have a proper deed drawn up about the money. I had his promise. One supposes that one can take the word of an English Peer. But I think that it's really all right. I have his letters about it."

"There's no saying. You'd better see a lawyer about it and find out. But this isn't a very dark past," he said, and rose and came to her and kissed her.

He was, indeed, relieved and reassured. In these circumstances the six hundred a year was not an allowance at all. It was merely the payment of a debt–a just debt.

"But it won't be nearly so nice for us, if the hog does manage to cut the six hundred down to three hundred. My husband only left me a hundred a year," she said, frowning.

"To be with you will be perfection, whatever our income is," said Mr. Manley, with ringing conviction, and he kissed her again.

She smiled happily and said: "He shan't cut it down. I'll see that he doesn't. When I've had a talk with him, he'll be glad enough to leave it as it is."

"It's very likely that he's only trying it on. It's the kind of thing he would do. But you'll find it difficult to get that talk. He's bent on shirking it," said Mr. Manley.

"I'll see that he doesn't get the chance of shirking it," she said, and her eyes gleamed again.

"I believe you're the only person in the world he's afraid of," he said in a tone of admiration.

"I shouldn't wonder," she said. "At any rate, I seem to be the only person in the world to whom he's always been civil. At least, I've never heard of anyone else."

"I'm afraid he won't be civil when you get that talk with him–if ever you do get it," said Mr. Manley, frowning rather anxiously.

"That'll be all the worse for him," she said dauntlessly. "But, after all, if I did fail to make him leave my income at six hundred, we should still have this house and four hundred a year. We should still be quite comfortable. Besides, you could keep on as his secretary, and that would be another two hundred a year."

"I can't do that! It's out of the question!" cried Mr. Manley. "I'm getting so to loathe the brute that I shall soon be quite unable to stand him. As it is, I sometimes have a violent desire to wring his neck. Now that I know that he played this measly trick on you, it will be more violent than ever. Besides, we must have a flat in town. It's really necessary to my work! I can do my actual writing down here fairly well. But what I really need is to get in touch with the right people, with the people who are really stimulating. Besides, I'm gregarious; I like mixing with people."

"Yes. You're right. We must have a flat in town. Therefore, I must make the hog keep to his bargain, and I will," she said firmly.

"I believe you may," he said, gazing at her determined face with admiring eyes.

There was a pause. Then she said carelessly: "When are we going to tell people that we're engaged?"

"Not yet awhile," said Mr. Manley quickly. "At least I don't want the people about here to know about it. And if you come to think of it, things being as they are, Loudwater would probably make himself more infernally disagreeable to me than he does at present. He'd not only try to take it out of me to annoy you, but it's just as likely as not that he would consider my getting engaged to you as poaching on his preserves–infernal cheek. He's the most hopelessly vain and unreasonable sweep in the British Isles."

"I shouldn't be a bit surprised if he did. He couldn't possibly help being a dog in the manger," she said thoughtfully. "And there's another thing. It has just occurred to me that if he tries to halve my income for nothing at all, he might try to stop it altogether if I got married. No; I must get that matter settled for good and all. I'll have that talk with him at once."

"If you can get it," said Mr. Manley doubtfully.

"I can get it," she said confidently. "You must remember that, having lived here for nearly two years, I know all about his habits. I shall take him by surprise. But we've talked enough about these dull things; let's talk about something interesting. How's the play going?"

They talked about the play he was writing, and then they talked about one another. They had their afternoon tea soon after four, for Mr. Manley had to return to the Castle to deal with any letters that the five o'clock post might bring.

At twenty minutes to five he left Mrs. Truslove and walked back to the Castle. He was truly in love with Helena. She was intelligent and appreciative. She was of his own class, with his own practical outlook on life, born of having belonged to a middle-class family of moderate means like himself. She was the daughter of a country architect. He could nowhere have found a more suitable wife. He was relieved about the matter of the reason why she received an allowance from Lord Loudwater; but he was not relieved about the matter of its being halved. Seven hundred a year had been an excellent income for the wife of a struggling playwright to enjoy. It had promised him the full social life in which his genius would most rapidly develop. He had regarded that income with great pleasure. Ever since Lord Loudwater had bidden him inform Helena of his intention of halving her allowance he had been bitterly angered by this barefaced attempt to rob her and consequently her future husband. In the light of her story the attempt had grown yet more disgraceful, and he resented it yet more bitterly.

The further danger that Lord Loudwater might attempt to stop her income altogether if she married, though he perceived that it was a real, even imminent danger, did not greatly trouble him. He was full of resentment, not fear. He felt that he loathed his employer more than ever and with more reason.

Holloway brought the post-bag to the library, and waited while Mr. Manley sorted the letters, that he might take those addressed to Lady Loudwater to her rooms and those addressed to the servants to the housekeeper's room.

As Mr. Manley inverted the bag and poured its contents on to the table, the footman said: "'Utchings 'as gone, sir."

"We must bear up," said Mr. Manley, in a tone wholly void of any sympathy with Hutchings in his misfortune.

"He was that furious. The things 'e said 'e'd do to his lordship!" said Holloway in a deeply-impressed tone.

"Threatened men live long," said Mr. Manley carelessly.

3

There is in the collection of the Earl of Ellesmere a picture of the head of a girl which the connoisseurs of the nineteenth century ascribed to Leonardo da Vinci. The connoisseurs of the twentieth century ascribe it to Luini. But for the colour of the hair it might have been a portrait of Lady Loudwater, a faded portrait. It might also very well be a portrait of one of her actual ancestresses, for her grandmother was a lady of an old Tuscan family.

Be that as it may, Lady Loudwater had the soft, dark, dreamy eyes, set rather wide apart, the straight, delicate nose, the alluring lips, promising all the kisses, the broad, well-moulded forehead, and the faint, exactly curving eyebrows of the girl in the picture. Above all, when Lord Loudwater was not present, the mysterious, enchanting, lingering smile, which is perhaps the chief charm of Luini's women, rested nearly always on her face. But while the hair of the girl in the picture is a deep, dull red, the hair of Olivia was dark brown with glimmers of gold in it. Also, her colouring was warmer than that of the girl in the picture, and her alluring charm stronger.

At a quarter to three that afternoon she came out on to the East lawn in a silk frock and hat of a green rather sombre for the summer day. She had been bidden by a fashionable fortune-teller never to wear green, for it was her unlucky colour. But that tint had so given her colouring its full values and her dark, liquid eyes so deep a depth, that she had paid no heed to the warning. There was a bright light of expectation in her eyes, and the alluring smile lingered on her face.

She walked quickly across the lawn with the easy, graceful gait proper to the accomplished golfer she was, into the shrubbery on the other side of it. A few feet along the path through it she looked sharply back over her shoulder. She saw no one at those windows of the East wing which looked on to the lawn and shrubbery, but a movement on the lawn itself caught her eye. The cat Melchisidec was following her. She did not slacken her pace, but for a moment the smile faded from her face at the remembrance of her husband's outburst at breakfast. Then the smile returned, subtile and expectant.

She did not wait for Melchisidec. She knew his way of pretending to follow her like a dog; she knew that if she displayed any interest in him, even showed that she was aware of his presence, he would probably come no further. She went on at the same brisk pace till she came to the gate in the East wood. She went through it, shut it gently, paused, and again looked back. All of the path through the shrubbery that she could see was empty. She turned and walked briskly along the narrow path through the wood, and came into the long, turf-paved aisle which ran at right angles to it.

The middle of the aisle was deeply rutted by the wheels of the carts which had carried away the timber from the spring thinning of the wood. She turned to the left and sauntered slowly up the smooth turf along the side of the aisle, a brighter light of expectation in her eyes, her smile even more mysterious and alluring.

She had not gone fifty yards up the aisle when Colonel Grey came limping out of the entrance of a path on the other side of it, and quickened his pace as he crossed it.

She stood still, flushing faintly, gazing at him with her lips parted a little. He looked, as he was, very young to be a Lieutenant-Colonel, and uncommonly fragile for a V. C. At any time he would look delicate, and he was the paler for the fact that at times he still suffered considerable pain from his wound. But there was force in his delicate, distinguished face. His sensitive lips could set very firm; his chin was square; his nose had a rather heavy bridge, and usually his grey eyes were cold and very keen. He gave the impression of being wrought of finely-tempered steel.

His eyes were shining so brightly at the moment that they had lost their keenness with their coldness. He marked joyfully the flush on her face, and did not know that he was flushing himself.

About five feet away he stopped, gazing, or rather staring, at her, and said in a tone of fervent conviction: "Heavens, Olivia! What a beautiful and entrancing creature you are!"

She smiled, flushing more deeply. He stepped forward, took her hand, and held it very tightly.

"Goodness! But I have been impatient for you to come!" he cried.

"I'm not late," she said in her low, sweet, rather drawling voice.

He let go of her hand and said: "I don't know how it is, but I've been as restless as a cat all the morning. I'm never sure that you will be able to come; and the uncertainty worries me."

"But you saw me for three hours yesterday," she said, moving forward.

"Yesterday?" he said, falling into step with her. "Yesterday is a thousand years away. I wasn't sure that you'd come today."

"Why shouldn't I come?" she said.

"Loudwater might have got to know of it and stopped you coming."

"Fortunately he doesn't take enough interest in my doings. Of course, if I didn't turn up at a meal, he'd make a fuss, though why he should make such a point of our having all our meals together I can't conceive. I should certainly enjoy mine much more if I had them in my sitting-room," she said in a dispassionate tone, for all the world as if she were discussing the case of someone else.

"I *am* so worried about you," he said with a harassed air. "Ever since that evening I heard him bullying you I've been simply worried to death about it."

"It was nice of you to interfere, but it was a pity," she said gently. "It didn't do any good as far as his behaviour is concerned, and we saw so much more of one another when you could come to the Castle."

"Then you do want to see more of me?" he said eagerly.

Lady Loudwater lost her smiling air; she became demureness itself, and she said: "Well, you see–thanks to Egbert's vile temper–we have so few friends."

Grey frowned; she was always quick to elude him. Then he growled: "What a name! Egbert!"

"He can't help that. It was given him. Besides, it's a family name," she said in a tone of fine impartiality.

"It would be. Hogbert!" said Grey contemptuously.

Mrs. Truslove and Mr. Manley were not the only people to ignore the essential bullness of Lord Loudwater.

They went on a few steps in silence; then she said: "Besides, I don't mind his outbursts. I'm used to them."

"I don't believe it! You're much too delicate and sensitive!" he cried.

"But I *am* getting used to them," she protested.

"You never will. Has he been bullying you again?" he said, looking anxiously into her eyes.

"Not more than usual," she said in a wholly indifferent tone.

"Then it is usual! I was afraid it was," he said in a miserable voice. "What on earth is to be done about it?"

"Why, there's nothing to be done, except just grin and bear it," she said bravely enough, and with the conviction of one who has thought a matter out thoroughly.

"Then it's monstrous! Just monstrous, that the most charming and loveliest creature in the world should be bullied by that infernal brute!" he cried, and put his arm around her.

The Countess was on the very point of slipping out of it when the cat Melchisidec came out of the bushes a dozen yards ahead of them, and with Melchisidec came a very distinct vision of Lord Loudwater's flushed, distorted, and revolting face as he swore at her at breakfast that morning.

She did not slip out of the encircling arm, and Grey bent his head and kissed her lightly on the lips.

It was the gentlest, lightest kiss, the kiss he might have given a pretty child, just a natural tribute to beauty and charm.

But the harm was done. The population of Great Britain cannot really be more than one and a half persons to the acre, and the great majority of them live, thousands to the acre, in towns; yet it is indeed difficult to kiss a girl during the daytime in any given acre, however thickly wooded, without being seen by some superfluous sojourner on that acre; and whether, or no, it was that the green frock and hat brought the Countess the bad luck the fortuneteller had foretold, there was a witness to that kiss.

Undoubtedly, too, it was not the right kind of witness. If it had been an indulgent elder not given to gossip, or a chivalrous young man not averse himself from kisses, all might have been well. But William Roper, under-gamekeeper, was a young man without a spark of chivalry in him, and he had been soured in the matter of kisses by the steadfast resolve of the young women of the village to suffer none from him. He was an unattractive young man, not unlike the ferrets he kept at his cottage. He was the last young man in the world, or at any rate in the neighbourhood, to keep silent about what he had seen.

Even so, no great harm might have been done. He might have blabbed about the matter in the village, and the whole village and the servants of the Castle might have talked about it for weeks and months, or even years, without it reaching the ears of Lord Loudwater. But William Roper saw in that kiss his royal road to Fortune. Ambitious in the grain, he was not content with his post of under-gamekeeper; he desired to oust William Hutchings from the post of head-gamekeeper, and though there were two under-gamekeepers senior to him with a greater claim on that post, occupy it himself. Here was the way to it; his lordship could not but be grateful to the man who informed him of such goings-on; he could not but promote him to the post of his desire.

He wholly misjudged his lordship. Ordinary gratitude was not one of his attributes.

Olivia slipped out of Grey's arm, and they walked on up the aisle. But they walked on, changed creatures—trembling, a little bemused.

William Roper, the ill-favoured minister of Nemesis, followed them.

At the top of the aisle they came to the pavilion, a small white marble building in the Classic style, standing in the middle of a broad glade.

As they went into it, Olivia said wistfully: "It's a pity I couldn't have tea sent here."

"I did. At least I brought it," said Grey, waving his hand towards a basket which stood on the table. "I knew you'd be happier for tea."

"No one has ever been so thoughtful of me as you are," she said, gazing at him with grateful, troubled eyes.

"Let's hope that your luck is changing," he said gravely, gazing at her with eyes no less troubled.

Then Melchisidec scratched at the door and mewed. Olivia let him in. Purring in the friendliest way, he rubbed his head against Grey's leg. He never treated Lord Loudwater with such friendliness.

William Roper chose a tree about forty yards from the pavilion and set his gun against the trunk. Then he filled and lit his pipe, leaned back comfortably against the trunk, hidden by the fringe of undergrowth, and, with his eyes on the door of the pavilion, waited. For Grey and

Olivia, never dreaming of this patient watcher, the minutes flew; they had so many things to tell one another, so many questions to ask. At least Grey had; Olivia, for the most part, listened without comment, unless the flush which waxed and waned should be considered comment, to the things he told her about herself and the many ways in which she affected him. For William Roper the minutes dragged; he was eager to start briskly up the royal road to Fortune. He was a slow smoker and he smoked a strong, slow-burning twist; but he had nearly emptied the screw of paper which held it before they came out of the door of the pavilion.

It was a still evening, but some drift of air had carried the rank smoke from William Roper's pipe into the glade, and it hung there. Colonel Grey had not taken five steps before his nostrils were assailed by it.

"Damn!" he said softly.

"What's the matter?" said Olivia.

She was too deeply absorbed in Grey for her senses to be alert, and the reek of William Roper's twist had reached her nostrils, but not her brain.

"There's someone about," he said. "Can't you smell his vile tobacco?"

"Bother!" said Olivia softly, and she frowned. They walked quietly on. Grey was careful not to look about him with any show of earnestness, for there was nothing to be gained by letting the watcher know that they had perceived his presence. Indeed, he would have seen nothing, for the undergrowth between him and the glade was too thin to form a good screen, and William Roper was now behind the tree-trunk.

Thirty yards down the broad aisle Grey said in a low voice: "This is an infernal nuisance!"

"Why?" said Olivia.

"If it comes to Loudwater's ears, he'll make himself devilishly unpleasant to you."

"He can't make himself more unpleasant than he does," she said, in a tone of quiet certitude and utter indifference. "But why shouldn't I have tea with you in the pavilion? It's what it's there for."

"All the same, Loudwater will make an infernal fuss about it, if it gets to his ears. He'll bully you worse than ever," he said in an unhappy tone, frowning heavily.

"What do I care about Loudwater—now?" she said, smiling at him, and she brushed her fingertips across the back of his hand.

He caught her fingers and held them for a moment, but the frown did not lift.

"The nuisance is that, whoever it was, he had been there a long time," he said gravely. "The glade was full of the reek of his vile tobacco. Suppose he saw me kiss you in the drive here and then followed us?"

"Well, if you will do such wicked things in the open air—" she said, smiling.

"It isn't a laughing matter, I'm afraid," he said rather heavily, and frowning.

"Well, I should have to consider your reputation and say that you didn't. It would be very bad for your career if it became known that you did such things, and Egbert would never rest till he had done everything he could do to injure you. I should certainly declare that you didn't, and you'd have to do the same."

"Oh, leave me out of it! Hogbert can't touch me. It's you I'm thinking about," he said.

"But there's no need to worry about me. I'm not afraid of Egbert any longer," she said, and her eyes, full of confidence and courage, met his steadily. Then, resolved to clear the anxiety away from his mind, she went on: "It's no use meeting trouble half-way. If someone did see us, Egbert may not get to hear of it for days, or weeks—perhaps never."

She did not know that they had to reckon with the ambition of William Roper.

"Lord, how I want to kiss you again!" he cried.

"You'll have to wait till tomorrow," she said.

It was as well that he did not kiss her again, for fifty yards behind them, stealing through the wood, came William Roper, all eyes. And he had already quite enough to tell.

Grey walked with her through the rest of the wood and nearly to the end of the path through the shrubbery. She spared no effort to set his mind at ease, protesting that she did not care a rap how furiously her husband abused her. A few yards from the edge of the East lawn they stopped, but they lingered over their parting. She promised to meet him in the East wood at three on the morrow.

She walked slowly across the lawn and up to her suite of rooms, thinking of Grey. She changed into a *peignoir*, lit a cigarette, lay down on a couch, and went on thinking about him. She gave no thought to the matter of whether they had been watched. Lord Loudwater had become of less interest than ever to her; his furies seemed trivial. She had a feeling that he had become a mere shadow in her life.

As she lay smoking that cigarette William Roper was telling his story to Lord Loudwater. He had waited in the wood till Colonel Grey had gone back through it; then he had walked briskly to the back door of the Castle and asked to see his lordship. Mary Hutchings, the second housemaid, who had answered his knock, took him to the servants' hall, and told Holloway what he asked. Both of them regarded him curiously; they themselves never wanted to see his lordship, though seeing him was part of their jobs, and one who could go out of his way to see him must indeed be remarkable. William Roper was hardly remarkable. He was merely somewhat repulsive. Holloway said that he would inquire whether his lordship would see him, and went.

As he went out of the door William Roper said, with an air of great importance: "Tell 'is lordship as it's very partic'ler."

Mary Hutchings' curiosity was aroused, and she tried to discover what it was. All she gained by doing so was an acute irritation of her curiosity. William Roper grew mysterious to the very limits of aggravation, but he told her nothing.

Her irritation was not alleviated when he said darkly: "You'll 'ear all about these goings-on in time."

She wished to hear all about them then and there.

Holloway came back presently, looking rather sulky, and said that his lordship would see William Roper.

"Though why 'e should curse me because you want to see 'im very partic'ler, I can't see," he added, with an aggrieved air.

He led the way, and for the first time in his life William Roper found himself entering the presence of the head of the House of Loudwater without any sense of trepidation. He carried himself unusually upright with an air of conscious rectitude.

Lord Loudwater was in the smoking-room in which he had that morning dealt with his letters with Mr. Manley. It was his favourite room, his smoking-room, his reading-room, and his office. He had been for a long ride, and was now lying back in an easy chair, with a long whisky-and-soda by his side, reading the *Pall Mall Gazette*. In literature his taste was blameless.

Holloway, ushering William Roper into the room, said: "William Roper, m'lord," and withdrew.

Lord Loudwater went on reading the paragraph he had just begun. William Roper gazed at him without any weakening of his courage, so strong was his conviction of the nobility of the duty he was discharging, and cleared his throat.

Lord Loudwater finished the paragraph, scowled at the interrupter, and said: "Well, what is it? Hey? What do you want?"

"It's about 'er ladyship, your lordship. I thought your lordship oughter be told about it—its not being at all the sort of thing as your lordship would be likely to 'old with."

There are noblemen who would, on the instant, have bidden William Roper go to the devil. Lord Loudwater was not of these. He set the newspaper down beside the whisky-and-soda, leaned forward, and said in a hushed voice: "What the devil are you talking about? Hey?"

"I seed Colonel Grey—the gentleman as is staying at the 'Cart and 'Orses'—kiss 'er in the East wood," said William Roper.

The first emotion of Lord Loudwater was incredulous amazement. It was his very strong conviction that his wife was a cold-blooded, passionless creature, incapable of inspiring or feeling any warm emotion. He had forgotten that he had married her for love—violent love.

"You infernal liar!" he said in a rather breathless voice.

"It ain't no lie, your lordship. What for should I go telling lies about 'er?" said William Roper in an injured tone.

Lord Loudwater stared at him. The fellow was telling the truth.

"And what did she do? Hey? Did she smack his face for him?" he cried.

"No. She let 'im do it, your lordship."

"She did?" bellowed his lordship.

"Yes. She didn't seem a bit put out, your lordship," said William Roper simply.

"And what happened then?" bellowed Lord Loudwater, and he got to his feet.

"They walked on to the pavilion, your lordship. An' they had their tea there. Leastways, I seed 'er ladyship come to the door an' empty hot water out of a tea-pot."

"Tea? Tea?" said Lord Loudwater in the tone of one saying: "Arson! Arson!"

Then, in all his black wrath, he perceived that he must have himself in hand to deal with the matter. He took a long draught of whisky-and-soda, rose, walked across the room and back again, grinding his teeth, rolling his eyes, and snapping the middle finger and thumb of his right hand. Never had the flush of rage been so deep in his face. It was almost purple. Never had his eyes protruded so far from his head.

He stopped and said thickly: "How long were they in the pavilion?"

"In the pavilion, your lordship? They were there a longish while—an hour and a half maybe," said William Roper, with quiet pride in the impression his information had made on his employer.

His employer looked at him as if it was the dearest wish of his heart to shake the life out of him then and there. It *was* the dearest wish of his heart. But he refrained. It would be a senseless act to slay the goose which lay these golden eggs of information.

"All right. Get out! And keep your tongue between your teeth, or I'll cut it out for you! Do you understand? Hey?" he roared, approaching William Roper with an air so menacing that the conscientious fellow backed against the door with his arm up to shield his face.

"I ain't a-going to say a word to no one!" he cried.

"You'd better not! Get out!" snarled his employer.

William Roper got out. Trembling and perspiring freely, he walked straight through the Castle and out of the back door without pausing to say a word to anyone, though he heard the voice of Holloway discussing his mysterious errand with Mary Hutchings in the servants' hall. He had walked nearly a mile before he succeeded in convincing himself that his feet were firmly set on the royal road to Fortune. His conviction was ill-founded.

4

For a good three minutes after the departure of William Roper the Lord Loudwater walked up and down the smoking-room. His redly-glinting eyes still rolled in a terrifying fashion, and still every few seconds he snapped his fingers in the throes of an effort to make up his raging mind whether to begin by an attack on his wife or on Colonel Grey. He could not remember ever having been so angry in his life; now and again his red eyes saw red.

Then of a sudden he made up his mind that he was at the moment angrier with Colonel Grey. He would deal with him first. Olivia could wait. He hurried out to the stables and bellowed for a horse with such violence that two startled grooms saddled one for him in little more than a minute.

He made no attempt to think what he would say to Colonel Grey. He was too angry. He galloped the two miles to the "Cart and Horses" at Bellingham, where Colonel Grey was staying, in order to restore his health and to fish.

At the door of the inn he bellowed: "Ostler! Ostler!" Then without waiting to see whether an ostler came, he threw the reins on his horse's neck, left it to its own devices, strode into the tap-room, and bellowed to the affrighted landlady, Mrs. Turnbull, to take him straight to Colonel Grey. Trembling, she led him upstairs to Grey's sitting-room on the first floor. Before she could knock, he opened the door, bounced through it, and slammed it.

Grey was sitting at the other side of the table, looking through a book of flies. He appeared to be quite unmoved by the sudden entry of the infuriated nobleman, or by his raucous bellow:

"So here you are, you infernal scoundrel!"

He looked at him with a cold, distasteful eye, and said in a clear, very unpleasant voice: "Another time knock before you come into my room."

Lord Loudwater had not expected to be received in this fashion; dimly he had seen Grey cowering.

He paused, then said less loudly: "Knock? Hey? Knock? Knock at the door of an infernal scoundrel like you?" His voice began to gather volume again. "Likely I should take the trouble! I know all about your scoundrelly game."

Colonel Grey remembered that Olivia had said that she proposed to deny the kiss, and his course was quite clear to him.

"I don't know whether you're drunk, or mad," he said in a quiet, contemptuous voice.

This again was not what Lord Loudwater had expected. But Grey was a strong believer in the theory that the attacker has the advantage, and he had an even stronger belief that an enemy in a fury is far less dangerous than an enemy calm.

"You're lying! You know I'm neither!" bellowed Lord Loudwater. "You kissed Olivia–Lady Loudwater–in the East wood. You know you did. You were seen doing it."

"You're raving, man," said Colonel Grey quietly, in a yet more unpleasant tone.

The interview was not going as Lord Loudwater had seen it. He had to swallow violently before he could say: "You were seen doing it! Seen! By one of my gamekeepers!"

"You must have paid him to say so," said Colonel Grey with quiet conviction.

Lord Loudwater was a little staggered by the accusation. He gasped and stuttered: "D-D-Damn your impudence! P-P-Paid to say it!"

"Yes, paid," said Colonel Grey, without raising his voice. "You happened to hear that we had tea in the pavilion in the wood–probably from Lady Loudwater herself–and you made up this stupid lie and paid your gamekeeper to tell it in order to score off her. It's exactly the dog's trick a bullying ruffian like you would play a woman."

"D-D-Dog's trick? Me?" stammered Lord Loudwater, gasping.

He was used to saying things of this kind to other people; not to have them said to him.

"Yes, you. You know that you're a wretched bully and cad," said Colonel Grey, with just a little more warmth in his tone.

Had Lord Loudwater's belief that William Roper had told him the truth about the kiss been weaker, it might have been shaken by the whole-hearted thoroughness of Grey's attack. But William Roper had impressed that belief on him deeply. He was sure that Grey had kissed Lady Loudwater.

The certainty spurred him to a fresh effort, and he cried: "It's no good your trying to humbug me–none at all. I've got evidence–plenty of evidence! And I'm going to act on it, too. I'm going to hound you out of the Army and that jade of a wife of mine out of decent society. Do you think, because I don't spend four or five months every year in that rotten hole, London, I haven't got any influence? Hey? If you do, you're damn well wrong. I've got more than enough twice over to clear a scoundrel like you out of the Army."

"Don't talk absurd nonsense!" said Grey calmly.

"Nonsense? Hey? Absurd nonsense?" howled Lord Loudwater on a new note of exasperation.

"Yes, nonsense. A disreputable cad like you can't hurt me in any way, and well you know it," said Grey with painstaking distinctness.

"Not hurt you? Hey? I can't hurt the corespondent in a divorce case? Hey?" said Lord Loudwater rather breathlessly.

"As if a man who has abused and bullied his wife as you have could get a divorce!" said Grey, and he laughed a gentle, contemptuous laugh, galling beyond words.

It galled Lord Loudwater surely enough; he snapped his fingers four times and gibbered.

"I tell you what it is: I've had enough of your manners," said Grey. "What you want is a lesson. And if I hear that you've been bullying Lady Loudwater about this simple matter of my having had tea with her, I'll give it you—with a horsewhip."

"You'll give me a lesson? You?" whispered Lord Loudwater, and he danced a little frantically.

"Yes. I'll give you the soundest thrashing any man hereabouts has had for the last twenty years, if I have to begin by knocking your ugly head off your shoulders," said Grey, raising his clear voice, so that for the first time Mrs. Turnbull, trembling, but thrilled, on the landing, heard what was being said.

The enunciation of Lord Loudwater had been thick, his words had been slurred.

"You? You thrash me?" he howled.

"Yes, me. Now get out!"

Lord Loudwater gnashed his teeth at him and again snapped his fingers. He burned to rush round the table and hammer the life out of Grey, but he could not do it; violent words, not violent deeds, were his accomplishment. Moreover, there was something daunting in Grey's cold and steady eye. He snapped his fingers again, and, pouring out a stream of furious abuse, turned to the door and flung out of it. Mrs. Turnbull scuttled aside into Grey's bedroom.

Half-way down the stairs Lord Loudwater paused to bellow: "I'll ruin you yet, you scoundrel! Mark my word! I *will* hound you out of the Army!"

He flung out of the house and found that the ostler had taken his horse round to the stable, removed its bridle, and given it a feed of corn. He cursed him heartily.

Grey rose, shut the door, and laughed gently. Then he frowned. Of a sudden he perceived that, natural as had been his manner of dealing with Lord Loudwater, he had handled him badly. At least, it was possible that he had handled him badly. It would have been wiser, perhaps, to have been suave and firm rather than firm and provoking. But it was not likely that suavity would have been of much use; the brute would probably have regarded it as weakness. But for Olivia's sake he ought probably to have tried to soothe him. As it was, the brute had gone raging off and would vent his fury on her.

What had he better do?

He was not long perceiving that there was nothing that he could do. The natural thing was to go to the Castle and prevent her husband—by force, if need be—from abusing and bullying Olivia. That was what his strongest instincts bade him do. It was quite impossible. It would compromise her beyond repair. He had done her harm enough by his impulsive indiscretion in the wood. His face slowly settled into a set scowl as he cudgelled his brains to find a way of coming effectually to her help. It seemed a vain effort, but a way had to be found.

Lord Loudwater galloped half-way to the Castle in a furious haste to punish Olivia for allowing Grey to make love to her, and even more for the contemptuous way in which Grey had treated him. He had hopes also of bullying her into a confession of the truth of William Roper's story. But Grey had excited him to a height of fury at which not even he could remain without exhaustion. In a reaction he reined in his horse to a canter, then to a trot, and then to a walk. He found that he was feeling tired.

He continued, however, to chafe at his injuries, but with less vehemence, and he was still resolved to make a strong effort to draw the confession from Olivia. On reaching the Castle, he did not go to her at once. He sat down in an easy chair in his smoking-room and drank two whiskies-and-sodas.

In the background of Olivia's mind, meditating pleasantly on her pleasant afternoon, there had been a patient and resigned expectation that presently her conscience would begin to reproach her for allowing Grey to make love to her. But the minutes slipped by, and she did not begin to feel that she had been wicked. The meditation remained pleasant. At last she realized suddenly that she was not going to feel wicked. She was surprised and even a trifle horror-stricken by her insensibility. Then, fairly faced by it, she came to the conclusion that, in a woman cursed with such a brute of a husband, such insensibility was not only natural, it was even proper.

Her woman's craving to be loved and to love was the strongest of her emotions, and it had gone unsatisfied for so long. Her husband had killed, or rather extirpated, her fondness for him before they had been married a month. She was inclined to believe that she had never really loved him at all. He had certainly ceased to love her before they had been married a fortnight, if, indeed, he had ever loved her at all. She had no child; she was an orphan without sisters or brothers. Her husband let her see but little of the friends who were fond of her. She began to suspect that her conscience did not reproach her because she had merely acted on her natural right to love and be loved. This conclusion brought her mind again to the consideration of Antony Grey, and again she let her thoughts dwell on him.

The gong, informing her that it was time to dress for dinner, interrupted this pleasant occupation. She had her bath, put herself into the hands of her maid, Elizabeth Twitcher, and resumed her meditation. She was at once so deeply absorbed in it that she did not observe her maid's sullen and depressed air.

She was presently interrupted again, and in a manner far more violent and startling than the summons of the gong. The door was jerked open, and her refreshed husband strode into the room.

"I know all about your little game, madam!" he cried. "You've been letting that blackguard Grey make love to you! You kissed him in the East wood this afternoon!"

The mysterious smile faded from the face of Olivia, and an expression of the most natural astonishment took its place.

"I sometimes think that you are quite mad, Egbert," she said in her slow, musical voice.

Elizabeth Twitcher continued her deft manipulation of a thick strand of hair without any change in her sullen and depressed air. To all seeming, she was uninterested, or deaf.

Lord Loudwater had expected, in the face of Olivia's gentleness, to have to work himself up to a proper height of indignant fury by degrees. The echo of Grey's accusation from the mouth of his wife raised him to it on the instant and without an effort.

"Don't lie to me!" he bellowed. "It's no good whatever! I tell you, I know!"

Olivia was surprised to find herself wholly free from her old fear of him. The fact that she was in love with Grey and he with her had already worked a change in her. These were the only things in the world of any real importance. That clear knowledge gave her a new confidence and a new strength. Her husband had been able to frighten her nearly out of her wits. Now he could not; and she could use them.

"I'm not lying at all. I really do believe you're mad— often," she said very distinctly.

Once more Lord Loudwater was compelled to grind his teeth. Then he laughed a harsh, barking laugh, and cried: "It's no good! I've just had a short interview with that scoundrel Grey. And I put the fear of God into him, I can tell you. I made him admit that you'd kissed him in the East wood."

For a breath Olivia was taken aback. Then she perceived clearly that it was a lie. He could not put the fear of God into Grey. Besides, Grey had kissed her, not she him.

"It's you who are lying," she said quickly and with spirit. "How could Colonel Grey admit a thing that never happened?"

Lord Loudwater perceived that it was going to be harder to wring the confession from her than he had expected. Checked, he paused. Then Elizabeth Twitcher caught his attention.

"Here: you—clear out!" he said.

Elizabeth Twitcher caught her mistress's eye in the glass. Olivia made no sign.

"I can't leave her ladyship's hair in this state, your lordship," said Elizabeth Twitcher with sullen firmness.

"You do as you're told and clear out!" bellowed his lordship.

"I don't want to be half an hour late for dinner," said Olivia, accepting the diversion and ready to make the most of it.

Elizabeth Twitcher looked at Lord Loudwater, saw more clearly than ever his likeness to the loathed James Hutchings, and made up her mind to do nothing that he bade her do. She went on dressing her mistress's hair sullenly.

"Are you going? Or am I to throw you out of the room?" cried Lord Loudwater in a blustering voice.

"Don't be silly, Egbert!" said Olivia sharply.

From the height of her new emotional experience she felt that her husband was merely a noisy and obnoxious boy. This was, indeed, quite plain to her. She felt years older than he and very much wiser.

Lord Loudwater, with a quite unusual glimmer of intelligence, perceived that bringing Elizabeth Twitcher into the matter had been a mistake. It had weakened his main action. In a less violent but more malevolent voice he said:

"Silly? Hey? I'll show you all about that, you little jade! You clear out of this first thing to-morrow morning. My lawyers will settle your hash for you. I'll deal with that blackguard Grey myself. I'll hound him out of the Army inside of a month. Perhaps it'll be a consolation to you to know that you've done him in as well as yourself."

He turned on his heel, left the room with a positively melodramatic stride, and slammed the door behind him.

Olivia was stricken by a sudden panic. She had lost all fear of her husband as far as she herself was concerned. He had become a mere offensive windbag. She did not care whether he did, or did not, try to divorce her. Even on the terms of so great a scandal it would be a cheap deliverance. But Antony was another matter.... She could not bear that he should be ruined on her account.... It was intolerable ... not to be thought of.... She must find some way of preventing it.

She began to cudgel her brains for that way of preventing it, but in vain. She could devise no plan. The more she considered the matter, the worse it grew. She could not bear to be associated in Antony's mind with disaster; she desired most keenly to stand foreverything that was pleasant and delightful in his life. She would not let her brute of a husband spoil both their lives. He had already spoiled enough of hers.

After his injunction to her to leave the Castle first thing next morning, she took it that they would hardly dine together, and told Elizabeth Twitcher to tell Wilkins to serve her dinner in her boudoir. Also, she refused to put on an evening gown, saying that the *peignoir* she was wearing was more comfortable on such a hot night. Last of all, she told her to pack some of her clothes that night.

Elizabeth Twitcher, stirred somewhat out of her brooding on her own troubles by this trouble of her mistress, looked at her thoughtfully and said: "I shouldn't go, m'lady. It'll look as if you agreed with what his lordship said. And it's only William Roper as has been telling these lies. He asked to see his lordship about something very partic'ler before his lordship went out. And who's going to pay any heed to William Roper?"

"William Roper? Who is William Roper? What kind of a man is he?" said Olivia quickly.

"He's an under-gamekeeper, m'lady, and the biggest little beast on the estate. Everybody hates William Roper," said Elizabeth with conviction.

This was satisfactory as far as it went. The worse her husband's evidence was the freer it left her to take her own course of action. But it was no great comfort, for she was but little concerned about the harm he could do her. Indeed, she was only concerned about the harm he could do Antony. She returned to her search for a method of preventing that harm during her dinner, and after her dinner she continued that search without any success. This injury to Antony, for her the central fact of the situation, weighed on her spirit more and more heavily.

The longer she pondered it the more harassed she grew. The most fantastic schemes for baulking her husband and saving Antony came thronging into her mind. She rose and walked restlessly up and down the room, working herself up into a veritable fever.

Mr. Manley, having dealt with the letters which had come by the five-o'clock post, read half a dozen chapters of the last published novel of Artzybachev with the pleasure he never failed to draw from the works of that author. Then he dressed and set forth, in a very cheerful spirit, to dine with Helena Truslove. His cheerful expectations were wholly fulfilled. She had divined that he was endowed, not only with a romantic spirit, but with a hearty and discriminating appetite, and was careful to give him good food and wine and plenty of both. With his coffee he smoked one of Lord Loudwater's favourite cigars. Expanding naturally, he talked with spirit and intelligence during dinner, and made love to her after dinner with even more spirit and intelligence. As a rule, he stayed on the nights he dined with her till a quarter to eleven. But that night she dismissed him at ten o'clock, saying that she was feeling tired and wished to go to bed early. Smoking another of Lord Loudwater's favourite cigars, he walked briskly back to the Castle, more firmly convinced than ever that every possible step must be taken to prevent any diminution of the income of a woman of such excellent taste in food and wine. It would be little short of a crime to discourage the exercise of her fine natural gift for stimulating the genius of a promising dramatist.

He was not in the habit of going to bed early, and having put on slippers and an old and comfortable coat, he once more turned to the novel by Artzybachev. He read two more chapters, smoking a pipe, and then he became aware that he was thirsty.

He could have mixed himself a whisky and soda then and there, for he had both in the cupboard, in his sitting-room. But he was a stickler for the proprieties: he had drunk red wine, Burgundy with his dinner and port after it, and after red wine brandy is the proper spirit. There would be brandy in the tantalus in the small dining-room.

He went quietly down the stairs. The big hall, lighted by a single electric bulb, was very dim, and he took it that, as was their habit, the servants had already gone to bed. As he came to the bottom of the stairs the door at the back of the hall opened; James Hutchings came through the doorway and shut the door quietly behind him.

Mr. Manley stood still. James Hutchings came very quietly down the hall, saw him, and started.

"Good evening, Hutchings. I thought you'd left us," said Mr. Manley, in a rather unpleasant tone.

"You may take your oath to it!" said James Hutchings truculently, in a much more unpleasant tone than Mr. Manley had used. "I just came back to get a box of cigarettes I left in the cupboard of my pantry. I don't want any help in smoking them from anyone here."

He opened the library door gently, went quietly through it, and drew it to behind him, leaving Mr. Manley frowning at it. It was a fact that Hutchings carried a packet, which might very well have been cigarettes; but Mr. Manley did not believe his story of his errand. He took it that he was leaving the Castle by one of the library windows. Well, it was no business of his.

At a few minutes past eight the next morning he was roused from the deep dreamless sleep which follows good food and good wine well digested, by a loud knocking on his door. It was not the loud, steady and prolonged knocking which the third housemaid found necessary to wake him. It was more vigorous and more staccato and jerkier. Also, a voice was calling loudly:

"Mr. Manley, sir! Mr. Manley! Mr. Manley!"

For all the noise and insistence of the calling Mr. Manley did not awake quickly. It took him a good minute to realize that he was Herbert Manley and in bed, and half a minute longer to gather that the knocking and calling were unusual and uncommonly urgent. He sat up in bed and yawned terrifically.

Then he slipped out of bed–the knocking and calling still continued–unlocked the door, and found Holloway, the second footman, on the threshold looking scared and horror-stricken.

"Please, sir, his lordship's dead!" he cried. "He's bin murdered! Stabbed through the 'eart!"

5

"Murdered? Lord Loudwater?" said Mr. Manley with another terrific yawn, and he rubbed his eyes. Then he awoke completely and said: "Send a groom for Black the constable at once. Yes–and tell Wilkins to telephone the news to the Chief Inspector at Low Wycombe. Hurry up! I'll get dressed and be down in a few minutes. Hurry up!"

Holloway turned to go.

"Stop!" said Mr. Manley. "Tell Wilkins to see that no one disturbs Lady Loudwater. I'll break the news myself when she is dressed."

"Yes, sir," said Holloway, and ran down the corridor.

Mr. Manley was much quicker than usual making his toilet, but thorough. He foresaw a hard and trying day before him, and he wished to start it fresh and clean. He would come into contact with new people; he saw himself playing an important role in a most important affair; he would naturally and as usual make himself valued. A slovenly air did not conduce to that. It seemed fitting to put on his darkest tweed suit and a black necktie.

When he came–briskly for him–downstairs he found a group of women servants in the hall, outside the door of the smoking-room, three of them snivelling, and Wilkins and Holloway in the smoking-room itself, standing and staring with a wholly helpless air at the body of Lord Loudwater, huddled in the easy chair in which he had been wont to sleep after dinner every evening.

"He's been stabbed, sir. There's that knife which was in the inkstand on the library table stickin' in 'is 'eart," said Wilkins in a dismal voice.

Mr. Manley glanced at the dead man. He looked to have been stabbed as he slept. His body had sagged down in the chair, and his head was sunk between his shoulders, so that he appeared almost neckless. His once so florid face was of an even, dead, yellowish pallor.

Mr. Manley's glance at the dead man was brief. Then he saw that the door between the smoking-room and the library was ajar. He could not see the library windows without crossing the smoking-room. That he would not do. He was a stickler for correctness in all matters, and he knew that the scene of a crime must be left untrampled.

He turned and said: "We will leave everything just as it is till the police come. And telephone at once to Doctor Thornhill, and ask him to come. If he is out, tell them to get word to him, Wilkins."

Wilkins and Holloway filed out of the room before him; he followed them out, locked the door and put the key in his pocket. Then he opened the door from the hall into the library. The long window nearest the smoking-room door was open.

The group of servants were all watching him; never had he moved or acted with an air of graver or greater importance. His portliness gave it weight.

"Has any of you opened the windows of the library this morning?" he said.

No one answered.

Then Mrs. Carruthers, the housekeeper, said: "Clarke does the library every morning. Have you done it this morning, Clarke?"

"No, mum. I hadn't finished the green droring-room when Mr. Holloway brought the sad news," said one of the housemaids.

Mr. Manley locked the library door and put that key also in his pocket.

Then he said in a tone of authority: "I think, Mrs. Carruthers, that the sooner we all have breakfast the better. I for one am going to have a hard day, and I shall need all my strength. We all shall."

"Certainly, Mr. Manley. You're quite right. We shall all need our strength. You shall have your breakfast at once. I'll have it sent to the little dining-room. You would like to be on the spot. Come along, girls. Wilkins, and you, Holloway, get on with your work as quickly as you can," said Mrs. Carruthers, driving her flock before her towards the servants' quarters.

"Thank you. And will you see that no one wakes Lady Loudwater before her usual hour, or tells her what has happened? I will tell her myself and try to break the news with as little of a shock as possible," said Mr. Manley.

"Twitcher hasn't bin downstairs yet. She doesn't know anything about it," said one of the maids.

"Send her straight to me—to the terrace when she does come down," said Mr. Manley, walking towards the hall door.

He felt that after the sight of the dead man's face the fresh morning air would do him good.

There came a sudden burst of excited chatter from the women as they passed beyond the door into the back of the Castle. All their tongues seemed to be loosed at once. Mr. Manley went out of the Castle door, crossed the drive, and walked up and down the lawn. He took long breaths through his nostrils; the sight of the dead man's yellowish face had been unpleasant indeed to a man of his sensibility.

In about five minutes Elizabeth Twitcher came out of the big door and across the lawn to him. She was looking startled and scared.

"Mrs. Carruthers said you wished to speak to me, sir?" she said quickly.

"Yes. I propose to break the news of this very shocking affair to Lady Loudwater myself. She's rather fragile, I fancy. And I think that it needs doing with the greatest possible tact—so as to lessen the shock," said Mr. Manley in an impressive voice.

Elizabeth Twitcher gazed at him with a growing suspicion in her eyes. Then she said: "It isn't—it isn't a trap?"

"A trap? What kind of a trap? What on earth do you mean?" said Mr. Manley, in a not unnatural bewilderment at the odd suggestion.

"You might be trying to take her off her guard," said Elizabeth Twitcher in a tone of deep suspicion.

"Her guard against what?" said Mr. Manley, still bewildered.

Elizabeth's Twitcher's eyes lost some of their suspicion, and he heard her breathe a faint sigh of relief.

"I thought as 'ow—as how some of them might have told you what his lordship was going to do to her, and that she—she stuck that knife into him so as to stop it," she said.

"What on earth are you talking about? What was his lordship going to do to her?" cried Mr. Manley, in a tone of yet greater bewilderment.

"He was going to divorce her ladyship. He told her so last night when I was doing her hair for dinner," said Elizabeth Twitcher.

She paused and stared at him, frowning. Then she went on: "And, like a fool, I went and talked about it—to someone else."

Mr. Manley glared at her in a momentary speechlessness; then found his voice and cried: "But, gracious heavens! You don't suspect her ladyship of having murdered Lord Loudwater?"

"No, I don't. But there'll be plenty as will," said Elizabeth Twitcher with conviction.

"It's absurd!" cried Mr. Manley.

Elizabeth Twitcher shook her head.

"You must allow as she had reason enough—for a lady, that is. He was always swearing at her and abusing her, and it isn't at all the kind of thing a lady can stand. And this divorce coming on the top of it all," she said in a dispassionate tone.

"You mustn't talk like this! There's no saying what trouble you may make!" cried Mr. Manley in a tone of stern severity.

"I'm not going to talk like that—only to you, sir. You're a gentleman, and it's safe. What I'm afraid of is that I've talked too much already—last night that is," she said despondently.

"Well, don't make it worse by talking any more. And let me know when your mistress is dressed, and I'll come up and break the news of this shocking affair to her."

"Very good, sir," said Elizabeth, and with a gloomy face and depressed air she went back into the Castle.

She had scarcely disappeared, when Holloway came out to tell Mr. Manley that his breakfast was ready for him in the little dining-room. Mr. Manley set about it with the firmness of a man preparing himself against a strenuous day. The frown with which Elizabeth Twitcher's suggestion had puckered his brow faded from it slowly, as the excellence of the chop he was eating soothed him. Holloway waited on him, and Mr. Manley asked him whether any of the servants had heard anything suspicious in the night. Holloway assured him that none of them had.

Mr. Manley had just helped himself a second time to eggs and bacon when Wilkins brought in Robert Black, the village constable. Mr. Manley had seen him in the village often enough, a portly, grave man, who regarded his position and work with the proper official seriousness. Mr. Manley told him that he had locked the door of the smoking-room and of the library, in order that the scene of the crime might be left undisturbed for examination by the Low Wycombe police. Robert Black did not appear pleased by this precaution. He would have liked to demonstrate his importance by making some preliminary investigations himself. Mr. Manley did not offer to hand the keys over to him. He intended to have the credit of the precautions he had taken with the constable's superiors.

He said: "I suppose you would like to question the servants to begin with. Take the constable to the servants' hall, give him a glass of beer, and let him get to work, Wilkins."

He spoke in the imperative tone proper to a man in charge of such an important affair, and Robert Black went. Mr. Manley could not see that the grave fellow could do any harm by his questions, or, for that matter, any good.

He finished his breakfast and lighted his pipe. Elizabeth Twitcher came to tell him that Lady Loudwater was dressed. He told her to tell her that he would like to see her, and followed her up the stairs. The maid went into Lady Loudwater's sitting-room, came out, and ushered him into it.

His strong sense of the fitness of things caused him to enter the room slowly, with an air grave to solemnity. Olivia greeted him with a faint, rather forced smile.

He thought that she was paler than usual, and lacked something of her wonted charm. She seemed rather nervous. She thought that he had come from her husband with an unpleasant and probably most insulting message.

He cleared his throat and said in the deep, grave voice he felt appropriate: "I've come on a very painful errand, Lady Loudwater—a very painful errand."

"Indeed?" she said, and looked at him with uneasy, anxious eyes.

"I'm sorry to tell you that Lord Loudwater has had an accident, a very bad accident," he said.

"An accident? Egbert?" she cried, in a tone of surprise that sounded genuine enough.

It gave Mr. Manley to understand that she had expected some other kind of painful communication— doubtless about the divorce Lord Loudwater had threatened. But he had composed a series of phrases leading up by a nice gradation to the final announcement, and he went on: "Yes. There is very little likelihood of his recovering from it."

Olivia looked at him queerly, hesitating. Then she said: "Do you mean that he's going to be a cripple for life?"

"I mean that he will not live to be a cripple," said Mr. Manley, pleased to insert a further phrase into his series.

"Is it as bad as that?" she said, in a tone which again gave Mr. Manley the impression that she was thinking of something else and had not realized the seriousness of his words.

"I'm sorry to say that it's worse than that. Lord Loudwater is dead," he said, in his deepest, most sympathetic voice.

"Dead?" she said, in a shocked tone which sounded to him rather forced.

"Murdered," he said.

"Murdered?" cried Olivia, and Mr. Manley had the feeling that there was less surprise than relief in her tone.

"I have sent for Dr. Thornhill and the police from Low Wycombe," he said. "They ought to have been here before this. And I am going to telegraph to Lord Loudwater's solicitors. You would like to have their help as soon as possible, I suppose. There seems nothing else to be done at the moment."

"Then you don't know who did it?" said Olivia.

Her tone did not display a very lively interest in the matter or any great dismay, and Mr. Manley felt somewhat disappointed. He had expected much more emotion from her than she was displaying, even though the death of her ill-tempered husband must be a considerable relief. He had expected her to be shocked and horror-stricken at first, before she realized that she had been relieved of a painful burden. But she seemed to him to be really less moved by the murder of her husband than she would have been, had the Lord Loudwater carried out his not infrequent threat of shooting, or hanging, or drowning the cat Melchisidec.

"No one so far seems to be able to throw any light at all on the crime," said Mr. Manley.

Olivia frowned thoughtfully, but seemed to have no more to say on the matter.

"Well, then, I'll telegraph to Paley and Carrington, and ask Mr. Carrington to come down," said Mr. Manley.

"Please," said Olivia.

Mr. Manley hesitated; then he said: "And I suppose that I'd better be getting someone to make arrangements about the funeral?"

"Please do everything you think necessary," said Olivia. "In fact, you'd better manage everything till Mr. Carrington comes. A man is much better at arranging important matters like this than a woman."

"You may rely on me," said Mr. Manley, with a reassuring air, and greatly pleased by this recognition of his capacity. "And allow me to assure you of my sincerest sympathy."

"Thank you," said Olivia, and then with more animation and interest she added: "And I suppose I shall want some black clothes."

"Shall I write to your dressmaker?" said Mr. Manley.

"No, thank you. I shall be able to tell her what I want better myself."

Mr. Manley withdrew in a pleasant temper. It was true that as a student of dramatic emotion he had been disappointed by the calmness with which Olivia had received the news of the murder; but she had instructed him to do everything he thought fit. He saw his way to controlling the situation, and ruling the Castle till someone with a better right should supersede him. He was halfway along the corridor before he realized that Olivia had asked no single question about the circumstance of the crime. Indifference could go no further. But–he paused, considering–was it indifference? Could she–could she have known already?

As he came down the stairs Wilkins opened the door of the big hall, and a man of medium height, wearing a tweed suit and carrying a soft hat and a heavy malacca cane, entered briskly. He looked about thirty. On his heels came a tall, thin police inspector in uniform.

Mr. Manley came forward, and the man in the tweed suit said: "My name is Flexen, George Flexen. I'm acting as Chief Constable. Major Arbuthnot is away for a month. I happened to be at the police station at Low Wycombe when your news came, and I thought it best to come myself. This is Inspector Perkins."

Mr. Manley introduced himself as the secretary of the murdered man, and with an air of quiet importance told Mr. Flexen that Lady Loudwater had put him in charge of the Castle till her lawyer came. Then he took the keys of the smoking-room and the library door from his pocket and said:

"I locked up the room in which the dead body is, and the library through which there is also access to it, leaving everything just as it was when the body was found. I do not think that any traces which the criminal has left, if, that is, he has left any, can have been obliterated."

He spoke with the quiet pride of a man who has done the right thing in an emergency.

"That's good," said Mr. Flexen, in a tone of warm approval. "It isn't often that we get a clear start like that. We'll examine these rooms at once."

Mr. Manley went to the door of the smoking-room and was about to unlock it, when Dr. Thornhill, a big, bluff man of fifty-five, bustled in. Mr. Manley introduced him to Mr. Flexen; then he unlocked the door and opened it.

The doctor was leading the way into the smoking-room when Mr. Flexen stepped smartly in front of him and said: "Please stay outside all of you. I'll make the examination myself first."

He spoke quietly, but in the tone of a man used to command.

"But, for anything we know, his lordship may still be alive," said Dr. Thornhill in a somewhat blustering tone, and pushing forward. "As his medical adviser, it's my duty to make sure at once."

"I'll tell you whether Lord Loudwater is alive or not. Don't let anyone cross the threshold, Perkins," said Mr. Flexen, with quiet decision.

Perkins laid a hand on the doctor's arm, and the doctor said: "A nice way of doing things! Arbuthnot would have given his first attention to his lordship!"

"I'm going to," said Mr. Flexen quietly.

He went to the dead man, looked in his pale face, lifted his hand, let it fall, and said: "Been dead hours."

Then he examined carefully the position of the knife. He was more than a minute over it. Then he drew it gingerly from the wound by the ring at the end of it. It was one of these Swedish knives, the blades of which are slipped into the handle when they are not being used.

"I think that's the knife that lay, open, in the big ink-stand in the library. We used it as a paper-knife, and to cut string with," said Mr. Manley, who was watching him with most careful attention.

"It may have some evidence on the handle," said Mr. Flexen, still holding it by the ring, and he drove the point of it into the pad of blotting paper on which Mr. Manley had been wont to write letters at the murdered man's dictation.

"And how am I to tell whether the wound was self-inflicted, or not?" cried the doctor in an aggrieved tone.

"If you will get some of the servants, you can remove the body to any room convenient and make your examination. It's a clean stab into the heart, and it looks to me as if the person who used that knife had some knowledge of anatomy. Most people who strike for the heart get the middle of the left lung," said Mr. Flexen.

So saying, he gently drew the easy chair, in which the body was huddled, nearer the door by its back. Mr. Manley bade Holloway fetch Wilkins and two of the grooms, and then, eager for hints of the actions of a detective, so useful to a dramatist, gave all his attention again to the proceedings of Mr. Flexen, who was down on one knee on the spot in which the chair had stood, studying the carpet round it. He rose and walked slowly towards the door which opened into the library, paused on the threshold to bid Perkins examine the chair and the clothes of the murdered man, and went into the library.

He was still in it when the footman and the grooms lifted the body of Lord Loudwater out of the chair, and carried it up to his bedroom. Mr. Manley stayed on the threshold of the smoking-room. His interest in the doings of Mr. Flexen forbade him leaving it to superintend decorously the removal of the body.

Presently Mr. Flexen came back, and as he walked round the room, examining the rest of it, especially the carpet, Mr. Manley studied the man himself, the detective type. He was about five feet eight, broad-shouldered out of proportion to that height, but thin. He had an uncommonly good forehead, a square, strong chin, a hooked nose and thin, set lips, which gave him a rather predatory air, belied rather by his pleasant blue eyes. The sun wrinkles round their corners and his sallow complexion gave Mr. Manley the impression that he had spent some years in the tropics and suffered for it.

When Mr. Flexen had examined the room, though Inspector Perkins had already done so, he felt round the cushions of the easy chair in which Lord Loudwater had been stabbed, found nothing, and stood beside it in quiet thought.

Then he looked at Mr. Manley and said: "The murderer must have been someone with whom Lord Loudwater was so familiar that he took no notice of his or her movements, for he came up to him from the front, or walked round the chair to the front of him, and stabbed him with a quite straightforward thrust. Lord Loudwater should have actually seen the knife—unless by any chance he was asleep."

"He was sure to be asleep," said Mr. Manley quickly. "He always did sleep in the evening—generally from the time he finished his cigar till he went to bed. I think he acquired the habit from coming back from hunting, tired and sleepy. Besides, I came down for a drink between eleven and twelve, and I'm almost sure I heard him snore. He snored like the devil."

"Slept every evening, did he? That puts a different complexion on the business," said Mr. Flexen. "The murderer need *not* have been anyone with whom he was familiar."

"No. He need not. But are you quite sure that the wound wasn't self-inflicted—that it wasn't a case of suicide?" said Mr. Manley.

"No, I'm not; and I don't think that that doctor—what's his name? Thornhill—can be sure either. But why should Lord Loudwater have committed suicide?"

"Well, he had found out, or thought he had found out, something about Lady Loudwater, and was threatening to start an action against her for divorce. At least, so her maid told me this morning. And as he wholly lacked balance, he might in a fury of jealousy have made away with himself," said Mr. Manley thoughtfully.

"Was he so fond of Lady Loudwater?" said Mr. Flexen in a somewhat doubtful tone.

He had heard stories about Lord Loudwater's treatment of his wife.

"He didn't show any great fondness for her, I'm bound to say. In fact, he was always bullying her. But he wouldn't need to be very fond of anyone to go crazy with jealousy about her. He was a man of strong passions and quite unbalanced. I suppose he had been so utterly spoilt as a child, a boy, and a young man, that he never acquired any power of self-control at all."

"M'm, I should have thought that in that case he'd have been more likely to murder the man," said Mr. Flexen.

"He was," said Mr. Manley in ready agreement. "But the other's always possible."

"Yes; one has to bear every possibility in mind," said Mr. Flexen. "I've heard that he was a bad-tempered man."

"He was the most unpleasant brute I ever came across in my life," said Mr. Manley with heartfelt conviction.

"Then he had enemies?" said Mr. Flexen.

"Scores, I should think. But, of course, I don't know. Only I can't conceive his having had a friend," said Mr. Manley in a tone of some bitterness.

"Then it's certainly a case with possibilities," said Mr. Flexen in a pleased tone. "But I expect that the solution will be quite simple. It generally is."

He said it rather sadly, as if he would have much preferred the solution to be difficult.

"Let's hope so. A big newspaper fuss will be detestable for Lady Loudwater. She's a charming creature," said Mr. Manley.

"So I've heard. Do you know who the man was that Loudwater was making a fuss about?"

"I haven't the slightest idea. Probably the maid, Elizabeth Twitcher, will be able to tell you," said Mr. Manley.

Mr. Flexen walked across the room and drew the knife out of the pad of blotting-paper by the ring in its handle, and studied it.

"I suppose this is the knife that was in the library? They're pretty common," he said.

Mr. Manley came to him, looked at it earnestly, and said: "That's it all right. I tried to sharpen it a day or two ago, so that it would sharpen a pencil. I generally leave my penknife in the waist-coat I'm not wearing. But I couldn't get it sharp enough. It's rotten steel."

"All of them are, but good enough for a stab," said Mr. Flexen.

6

Olivia had very little appetite for breakfast. It is to be doubted, indeed, whether she was aware of what she was eating. Elizabeth Twitcher hovered about her, solicitous, pressing her to eat more. She was fond of her mistress, and very uneasy lest she should have harmed her seriously by her careless gossiping the night before. But she was surprised by the exceedingly anxious and worried expression which dwelt on Olivia's face. Her air grew more and more harassed. The murder of her husband had doubtless been a shock, but he had been such a husband. Elizabeth Twitcher had expected her mistress to cry a little about his death, and then grow serene as she realized what a good riddance it was. But Olivia had not cried, and she showed no likelihood whatever of becoming serene.

At the end of her short breakfast she lit a cigarette, and began to pace up and down her sitting-room with a jerky, nervous gait, quite unlike her wonted graceful, easy, swinging walk. She had to relight her cigarette, and as she did so, Elizabeth Twitcher, who was clearing away the breakfast, perceived that her hands were shaking. There was plainly more in the matter than Elizabeth Twitcher had supposed, and she wondered, growing more and more uneasy.

When she went downstairs with the tray she learned that Dr. Thornhill was examining the wound which had caused the Lord Loudwater's death, and that Mr. Flexen and Inspector Perkins were questioning Wilkins. Talking to the other servants, she found of a sudden that she had reason for anxiety herself, and hurried back in a panic to her mistress's boudoir. She found Olivia still walking nervously up and down.

"The inspector and the gentleman who is acting Chief Constable are questioning the servants, m'lady," said Elizabeth.

Olivia stopped short and stared at her with rather scared eyes.

Then she said sharply: "Go down and learn what the servants have told them—all the servants—everything."

Her mistress's plainly greater anxiety eased a little Elizabeth Twitcher's own panic in the matter of James Hutchings, and she went down again to the servants' quarters.

Mr. Flexen and Inspector Perkins learnt nothing of importance from Wilkins; but he made it clearer to Mr. Flexen that the temper of the murdered man had indeed been abominable. Holloway, on the other hand, proved far more enlightening. From him they learnt that Hatchings had been discharged the day before without notice, and that he had uttered violent threats against his employer before he went. Also they learnt that Hatchings, who had left about four o'clock in the afternoon, had come back to the Castle at night. Jane Pittaway, an under-house-maid, had heard him talking to Elizabeth Twitcher in the blue drawing-room between eleven and half-past.

Mr. Flexen questioned Holloway at length, and learned that James Hatchings was a man of uncommonly violent temper; that it had been a matter of debate in the servants' hall whether his furies or those of their dead master were the worse. Then he dismissed Holloway, and sent for Jane Pittaway. A small, sharp-eyed, sharp-featured young woman, she was quite clear in her story. About eleven the night before she had gone into the great hall to bring away two vases full of flowers, to be emptied and washed next morning, and coming past the door of the blue drawing-room, had heard voices. She had listened and recognized the voices of Hutchings and Elizabeth Twitcher. No; she had not heard what they were saying. The door was too thick. But he seemed to be arguing with her. Yes; she had been surprised to find him in the house after he had gone off like that. Besides, everybody thought that he had jilted Elizabeth Twitcher and was keeping company with Mabel Evans, who had come home on a holiday from her place in London to her mother's in the village. No; she did not know how long he stayed. She minded her own business, but, if anyone asked her, she must say that he was more likely to murder someone than anyone she knew, for he had a worse temper than his lordship even, and bullied everyone he came near worse than his lordship. In fact, she had never been able to understand how Elizabeth Twitcher could stand him, though of course everyone knew that Elizabeth could always give as good as she got.

When Mr. Flexen thanked her and said that she might go, she displayed a desire to remain and give them her further views on the matter. But Inspector Perkins shooed her out of the room.

Then Wilkins came to say that Dr. Thornhill had finished his examination and would like to see them.

He came in with a somewhat dissatisfied air, sat down heavily in the chair the inspector pushed forward for him, and said in a dissatisfied tone:

"The blade pierced the left ventricle, about the middle, a good inch and a half. Death was practically instantaneous, of course."

"I took it that it must have been. The collapse had been so complete. I suppose the blade stopped the heart dead," said Mr. Flexen.

"Absolutely dead," said the doctor. "But the thing is that I can't swear to it that the wound was not self-inflicted. Knowing Lord Loudwater, I could swear to it morally. There isn't the ghost of a chance that he took his own life. But physically, his right hand might have driven that blade into his heart."

"I thought so myself, though of course I'm no expert," said Mr. Flexen. "And I agree with you when you say that you are morally certain that the wound was not self-inflicted. Those bad-tempered brutes may murder other people, but themselves never."

"Well, I've not your experience in crime, but I should say that you were right," said the doctor.

"All the same, the fact that you cannot swear that the wound was not self-inflicted will be of great help to the murderer, unless we get an absolute case against him," said Mr. Flexen.

"Well, I'm sure I hope you will. Lord Loudwater had a bad temper—an infernal temper, in fact. But that's no excuse for murdering him," said Dr. Thornhill.

"None whatever," said Mr. Flexen. "What about the inquest? I suppose we'd better have it as soon as possible."

"Yes. Tomorrow morning, if you can," said the doctor, rising.

"Very good. Send word to the coroner at once, Perkins. Don't go yourself. I shall want you here," said Mr. Flexen.

He shook hands with the doctor and bade him good-day. As Inspector Perkins went out of the room to send word to the coroner, he bade him send Elizabeth Twitcher to him.

She was not long coming, for, in obedience to Olivia's injunction, she was engaged in learning what the other servants knew, or thought they knew, about the murder.

When she came into the dining-room, Mr. Flexen's keen eyes examined her with greater care than he had given to the other servants. On Jane Pittaway's showing, she should prove an important witness. Now Elizabeth Twitcher was an uncommonly pretty girl, dark-eyed and dark-haired, and her forehead and chin and the way her eyes were set in her head showed considerable character. Mr. Flexen made up his mind on the instant that he was going to learn from Elizabeth Twitcher exactly what

Elizabeth Twitcher thought fit to tell him and no more, for all that he perceived that she was badly scared.

He did not beat about the bush; he said: "You had a conversation with James Hutchings last night, about eleven o'clock, in the blue drawing-room. Did you let him in?"

Elizabeth Twitcher's cheeks lost some more of their colour while he was speaking, and her eyes grew more scared. She hesitated for a moment; then she said:

"Yes. I let him in at the side door."

He had not missed her hesitation; he was sure that she was not telling the truth.

"How did you know he was at the side door?" he said.

She hesitated again. Then she said: "He whistled to me under my window just as I was going to bed."

Again he did not believe her.

"Did you let him out of the Castle?" he said.

"No, I didn't. He let himself out," she said quickly.

"Out of the side door?"

"How else would he go out?" she snapped.

"You don't know that he went out by the side door?" said Mr. Flexen.

Elizabeth hesitated again. Then she said sullenly: "No, I don't. I left him in the blue drawing-room."

"In a very bad temper?" said Mr. Flexen.

"I don't know what kind of a temper he was in," she said.

Mr. Flexen paused, looking at her thoughtfully. Then he said: "I'm told that you and he were engaged to be married, and that he broke the engagement off."

"*I* broke it off!" said Elizabeth angrily, and she drew herself up very stiff and frowning.

It was Mr. Flexen's turn to hesitate. Then he made a shot, and said: "I see. He wanted you to become engaged to him again, and you wouldn't."

Elizabeth looked at him with an air of surprise and respect, and said: "It wasn't quite like that, sir. I didn't say as I wouldn't be his fioncy again. I said I'd see how he behaved himself."

"Then he wasn't in a good temper," said Mr. Flexen.

"He was in a better temper than he'd any right to expect to be," said Elizabeth with some heat.

"That's true," said Mr. Flexen, smiling at her. "But after the trouble he had had with Lord Loudwater he couldn't be in a very good temper."

"He was too used to his lordship's tantrums to take much notice of them. He was too much that way himself," said Elizabeth quickly.

"I see," said Mr. Flexen. "What time was it when he left you?"

"I can't rightly say. But it wasn't half-past eleven," she said.

He perceived that that was true. At the moment there was no more to be learned from her. If she could throw any more light on the doings of James Hutchings, she was on her guard and would not. But he had learned that James Hutchings had not entered the Castle by the side door. Had he entered it and left it by the library window?

He asked Elizabeth a few more unimportant questions and dismissed her.

Inspector Perkins, having sent a groom to inform the coroner of the murder, and of the need for an early inquest into it, came back to him. They discussed the matter of James Hutchings, and decided to have him watched and arrest him on suspicion should he try to leave the neighbourhood. The inspector telephoned to Low Wycombe for two of his detectives.

Mr. Flexen questioned the rest of the servants and learned nothing new from them. By the time he had finished the two detectives from Low Wycombe arrived, and he sent them out to make inquiries in the village, though he thought it unlikely that anything was to be learnt there, unless Hutchings had been talking again.

He had risen and was about to go to the smoking-room to look round it again, on the chance that something had escaped his eye, when Mrs. Carruthers, the housekeeper, entered the room. None of the servants had mentioned her to him, and it had not occurred to him that there would of course be a housekeeper.

"Good morning, Mr. Flexen. I'm Mrs. Carruthers, the housekeeper," she said. "You didn't send for me. But I thought I ought to see you, for I know something which may be important, and I thought you ought to know it, too."

"Of course. I can't know too much about an affair like this," said Mr. Flexen quickly.

"Well, there was a woman, or rather I should say a lady, with his lordship in the smoking-room last night–about eleven o'clock."

"Indeed?" said Mr. Flexen. "Won't you sit down? A lady you say?"

"Yes; she was a lady, though she seemed very angry and excited, and was talking in a very high voice. I didn't recognize it, so I can't tell you who it was. You see, I don't belong to the neighbourhood. I've only been here six weeks."

"And how long did this interview last?" said Mr. Flexen.

"I can't tell you. It was no business of mine. I was making my round last thing to see that the servants had left nothing about. I always do. You know how careless they are. I went round the hall, and then I went to bed. But, of course, I wondered about it," said Mrs. Carruthers.

Mr. Flexen looked at her refined, rather delicate face, and he did not wonder how she had repressed her natural curiosity.

"Can you tell me whether the French window in the library, the end one, was open at that time?" he said.

"I can't," she said in a tone of regret. "I couldn't very well open the library door. If the door between the library and the smoking-room was open, I should have been certain to hear something that was not meant for my ears. And it generally is open in summer time. But I should think it very likely that the lady came in by that window. It's always open in summer time. In fact, his lordship always went out into the garden through it, going from his smoking-room."

"And what time was it that you heard this?" he said.

"A few minutes past eleven. I looked round the drawing-room and the two dining-rooms, and it was a quarter-past eleven when I came into my room."

"That's the first exact time I've got from anyone yet," said Mr. Flexen in a tone of satisfaction. "And that's all you heard?"

She hesitated, and a look of distress came over her face. Then she said: "You have questioned Elizabeth Twitcher. Did she tell you anything about his lordship's last quarrel with her ladyship?"

"She did not," said Mr. Flexen. "Mr. Manley told me that she had told him about the quarrel. But I did not question her about it. I left it till later."

Mrs. Carruthers hesitated; then she said: "It's so difficult to see what one's duty is in a case like this."

"Well, one's obvious duty is to make no secret of anything that may throw a light on the crime. Was it anything out of the way in the way of quarrels? Wasn't Lord Loudwater always quarrelling with Lady Loudwater? I've been told that he was always insulting and bullying her."

"Well, this one was rather out of the common," said Mrs. Carruthers reluctantly. "He accused her of having kissed Colonel Grey in the East wood and declared that he would divorce her."

"It was Colonel Grey, was it?" said Mr. Flexen.

"That is what Elizabeth Twitcher told me after supper last night. It seems that his lordship burst in upon them when she was dressing her ladyship's hair for dinner and blurted it out before her. I've no doubt she was telling the truth. Twitcher is a truthful girl."

"Moderately truthful," said Mr. Flexen in a somewhat ironical tone.

"Of course she may have exaggerated. Servants do," said Mrs. Carruthers.

"And how did Lady Loudwater take it?" said Mr. Flexen.

"Twitcher said that she denied everything, and did not appear at all upset about it. Of course, she was used to Lord Loudwater's making scenes. He had a most dreadful temper."

"M'm," said Mr. Flexen, and he played a tune on the table with his finger-tips, frowning thoughtfully. "Was Colonel Grey–I suppose it is Colonel Antony Grey–the V.C. who has been staying down here?"

"Yes," said Mrs. Carruthers. "He's at the 'Cart and Horses' at Bellingham."

"Was he on good terms with Lord Loudwater?"

"They were quite friendly up to about a fortnight ago. The Colonel used to play billiards with his lordship and stay on to dinner two or three times a week. Then they had a quarrel–about the way his lordship treated her ladyship. Holloway, the footman, heard it, and the Colonel told his lordship that he was a cad and a blackguard, and he hasn't been here since."

"But he met Lady Loudwater in the wood?"

"So his lordship declared," said Mrs. Carruthers in a non-committal tone.

"Do you know how Lord Loudwater came to hear of their meeting?"

"Twitcher said that he must have had it from one of the under-gamekeepers, a young fellow called William Roper. Roper asked to see his lordship that evening and was very mysterious about his errand, so that it looks as if she might be right. None of the servants ever went near his lordship, if they could help it. It had to be something very important to induce William Roper to go to him of his own accord."

"I see," said Mr. Flexen thoughtfully. "Well, I'm glad you told me about this. Do you suppose that this Twitcher girl has talked to anyone but you about it?"

"That I can't say at all. But she has a bedroom to herself," said Mrs. Carruthers. "Besides, if she had talked to any of the others, they would have told you about it."

"Yes; there is that. I think it would be a good thing if you were to give her a hint to keep it to herself. It may have no bearing whatever on the crime. It's not probable that it has. But it's the kind of thing to set people talking and do both Lady Loudwater and Colonel Grey a lot of harm."

"I will give her a hint at once," said Mrs. Carruthers, rising. "But the unfortunate thing is that if Twitcher doesn't talk, this young fellow Roper will. And, really, Lord Loudwater gave her ladyship quite enough trouble and unhappiness when he was alive without giving her more now that he's dead."

"I may be able to induce William Roper to hold his tongue," said Mr. Flexen dryly. "Certainly his talking cannot do any good in any case. And I have gathered that Lady Loudwater has suffered quite enough already from her husband."

"I'm sure she has; and I do hope you will be able to keep that young man quiet," said Mrs. Carruthers, moving towards the door. As she opened it, she paused and said: "Will you be here to lunch, Mr. Flexen?"

"To lunch and probably all the afternoon." He hesitated and added: "It would be rather an advantage if I could sleep here, too. I do not think that I shall need to look much further than the Castle for the solution of this problem, though there's no telling. At any rate, I should like to have exhausted all the possibilities of the Castle before I leave it. And if I'm on the spot, I shall probably exhaust them much more quickly."

"Oh, that can easily be arranged. I'll see her ladyship about it at once," said Mrs. Carruthers quickly.

"And would you ask her if she feels equal to seeing me yet?"

"Certainly, Mr. Flexen; and if she does, I'll let you know at once," she said and went through the door.

Mr. Flexen was considering the new facts she had given him, when about three minutes later Inspector Perkins returned; and Mr. Flexen bade him find William Roper and bring him to him without delay. The inspector departed briskly. He was not used to having the inquiry into a crime conducted by the Chief Constable himself; but Mr. Flexen had impressed the conviction on him that it was work which he thoroughly understood. Moreover, he had been appointed acting Chief Constable of the district during the absence of Major Arbuthnot, on the ground of his many years' experience in the Indian Police. Also, the inspector realized that this was, indeed, an exceptional case worthy of the personal effort of any Chief Constable. He could not remember a case of the murder of a peer; they had always seemed to him a class immune from anything more serious than ordinary assault. He was pleased that Mr. Flexen was conducting the inquiry himself, for he did not wish Scotland Yard to deal with it. Not only would that cast a slur on the capacity of the police of the district, but he was sure that he himself would get much more credit for his work, if he and Mr. Flexen were successful in discovering the murderer, than he would get if a detective inspector from Scotland Yard were in charge of the case. Such a detective inspector might or might not earn all the credit, but he would certainly know how to get it and probably insist on having it.

He had not been gone a minute when Elizabeth Twitcher came into the dining-room, said that her ladyship would be pleased to see Mr. Flexen, and led him upstairs to her sitting-room.

He found Olivia paler than her wont, but quite composed. She had lost her nervous air, for she had perceived very clearly that it would be dangerous, indeed, to display the anxiety which was harassing her. It was only natural that she should appear upset by the shock, but not that she should appear in any way fearful.

Mr. Flexen had been told that Lady Loudwater was pretty, but he had not been prepared to find her as charming a creature as Olivia. He made up his mind at once to do the best he could to save her from the trouble that the gossip about her and Colonel Grey would surely bring upon her–if always he were satisfied that neither of them had a hand in the crime. Looking at Olivia, nothing seemed more unlikely than that she should be in any way connected with it. But he preserved an open mind. As such reasons go, she was not without reasons, substantial reasons, for getting rid of her husband, and she appeared to him to be a creature of sufficiently delicate sensibilities to feel that husband's brutality more than most women. At the same time he found it hard to conceive of her using that fatal knife herself. Yet the knife is most frequently the womanly weapon.

For her part, Olivia liked his face; but she had an uneasy feeling that he would go further than most men in solving any problem with which he set his mind to grapple.

They greeted one another; he sat down in a chair facing the light, though he would have preferred that Olivia should have faced it, and expressed his concern at the trouble which had befallen her.

Then he said: "I came to see you, Lady Loudwater, in the hope that you might be able to throw some light on this deplorable event."

"I don't think I can," said Olivia gently. "But of course, if I can do anything to help you find out about it I shall be very pleased to try."

She looked at him with steady, candid eyes that deepened his feeling that she had had no hand in the crime.

"And, of course, I'll make it as little distressing for you as I can," he said. "Do you know whether your husband had anything worrying him–any serious trouble of any kind which would make him likely to commit suicide?"

"Suicide? Egbert?" cried Olivia, in a tone of such astonishment that, as far as Mr. Flexen was concerned, the hypothesis of suicide received its death-blow. "No. I don't know of anything which would have made him commit suicide."

"Of course he had no money troubles; but were there any domestic troubles which might have unhinged his mind to that extent?" said Mr. Flexen.

He wished to be able to deal with the hypothesis of suicide, should it be put forward.

Olivia did not answer immediately. She was thinking hard. The possibility that her husband had committed suicide, or that anyone could suppose that he had committed suicide, had never entered her head. She perceived, however, that it was a supposition worth encouraging. At the same time, she must not seem eager to encourage it.

"But they told me that he'd been murdered," she said.

"We cannot exclude any possibility from a matter like this, and the possibility of suicide must be taken into account," said Mr. Flexen quickly. "You don't know of any domestic trouble which might have induced Lord Loudwater to make an end of himself?"

"No, I don't know of one," said Olivia firmly. "But, of course, he was sometimes quite mad."

"Mad?" said Mr. Flexen.

"Yes, quite. I told him so last night–just before dinner. He was quite mad. He said that I had kissed a friend of ours–at least he was a friend of both of us till he quarrelled with my husband some weeks ago–in the East wood. He raged about it, and declared he was going to start a divorce action. But I didn't take much notice of it. He was always falling into dreadful rages. There was one at breakfast about my cat and another at lunch about the wine. He fancied it was corked."

Olivia had perceived clearly that since Elizabeth Twitcher had been a witness of her husband's outburst about Grey, it would be merely foolish not to be frank about it.

"But the last matter was very much more serious than the matter of the cat or the wine," said Mr. Flexen. "You don't think that your husband brooded on it for the rest of the evening and worked himself up into a dangerous frame of mind?"

Olivia hesitated. She was quite sure that her husband had done nothing of the kind, for if he had worked himself up into a dangerous frame of mind he would assuredly have made some effort to get at her and give some violent expression to it. But she said:

"That I can't say. I wish I'd gone down to dinner—now. But I was too much annoyed. I dined in my boudoir. I'd had quite enough unpleasantness for one day. Perhaps one of the servants could tell you. They may have noticed something unusual in him—perhaps that he was brooding."

"Wilkins did say that Lord Loudwater seemed upset at dinner, and that he was frowning most of the meal," said Mr. Flexen.

"That wasn't unusual," said Olivia somewhat pathetically. "Besides—"

She stopped short, on the very verge of saying that she was sure that those frowns cleared from her husband's face before the sweets, for he would never take afternoon tea, in order to have a better appetite for dinner, and consequently was wont to begin that meal in a tetchy humour. Such an explanation would have gone no way to support the hypothesis of suicide. Instead of making it she said:

"Of course, he did seem frightfully upset."

"But you don't think that he was sufficiently upset to do himself an injury?" said Mr. Flexen.

Olivia had formed a strong impression that her husband would not in any circumstance do himself an injury; it was his part to injure others. But she said:

"I can't say. He might have gone on working himself up all the evening. I didn't see him after he left my dressing-room. It was there he made the row—while I was dressing for dinner."

Mr. Flexen paused; then he said: "Mr. Manley tells me that Lord Loudwater used to sleep every evening after dinner. Do you think that he was too upset to go to sleep last night?"

"Oh, dear no! I've known him go to sleep in his smoking-room after a much worse row than that!" cried Olivia.

"With you?" said Mr. Flexen quickly.

"No; with Hutchings—the butler," said Olivia.

"But that wouldn't be such a serious matter—not one to brood upon," said Mr. Flexen.

"I suppose not," said Olivia readily.

Mr. Flexen paused again; then he said in a somewhat reluctant tone: "There's another matter I must go into. Have you any reason to believe that there was any other woman in Lord Loudwater's life—anything in the nature of an intrigue? It's not a pleasant question to have to ask, but it's really important."

"Oh, I don't expect any pleasantness where Lord Loudwater is concerned," said Olivia, with a sudden almost petulant impatience, for this inquisition was a much more severe strain on her than Mr. Flexen perceived. "Do you mean now, or before we were married?"

"Now," said Mr. Flexen.

"I haven't the slightest idea," said Olivia.

"Do you think it likely?" said Mr. Flexen.

"No, I don't—not very. I don't see how he could have got another woman in. He was always about—always. Of course, he rode a good deal, though."

"He did, did he?" said Mr. Flexen quickly.

"Every afternoon and most mornings."

That was important. Mr. Flexen thought that he might not have to go very far afield to find the woman who had been quarrelling with Lord Loudwater at a few minutes past eleven the night before. She probably lived within an easy ride of the Castle.

"I'm very much obliged to you for helping me so readily in such distressing circumstances," he said in a grateful voice as he rose. "If anything further occurs to you that may throw any light on the matter, you might let me hear it with as little delay as possible."

"I will," said Olivia. "By the way, Mrs. Carruthers told me that you would like to stay here while you were making your inquiry; please do; and please make any use of the servants and the cars you like. My husband's heir is still in Mesopotamia, and I expect that I shall have to run the Castle till he comes back."

"Thank you. To stay here will be very convenient and useful," said Mr. Flexen gratefully, and left her.

He came down the stairs thoughtfully. It seemed to him quite unlikely that she had had anything to do with the crime, or knew anything more about it than she had told him. Nevertheless, there was this business of Colonel Grey and her murdered husband's threat to divorce her. They must be borne in mind.

He would have been surprised, intrigued, and somewhat shaken in his conviction that she had been in no way connected with the murder, had he heard the gasp of intense relief which burst from Olivia's lips when the door closed behind him, and seen her huddle up in her chair and begin to cry weakly in the reaction from the strain of his inquisition.

7

Mr. Flexen found Inspector Perkins waiting for him in the dining-room with the information that James Hutchings was at his father's cottage in the West wood, and that he had set one of his detectives to watch him. Also, he told him that he had learned that Hutchings was generally disliked in the village as well as at the Castle, as a violent, bad-tempered man, with a habit of fixing quarrels on anyone who would quarrel with him, and as often as not on mild and inoffensive persons, quite incapable of bearing themselves in a quarrel with any unpleasant effectiveness.

Mr. Flexen discussed with the inspector the question of taking out a warrant for the arrest of Hutchings, and they decided that there was no need to take the step—at any rate, at the moment; it was enough to have him watched. He would learn doubtless that it was known that he had been in the Castle late the night before. If, on learning it, he took fright and bolted, it would rather simplify the case.

Then Mr. Flexen sent again for Elizabeth Twitcher and questioned her at length about Lord Loudwater's onslaught on Lady Loudwater the night before and about the condition in which he had been at the end of it. Elizabeth was somewhat sulky in her manner, for she felt that she was to blame for that onslaught having come to Mr. Flexen's ears. She was the more careful to make it plain that however violently Lord Loudwater may have been affected, Olivia had taken the business lightly enough, and decided to ignore his injunction to her to leave the Castle. Mr. Flexen did not miss the point that Lord Loudwater had threatened to hound Colonel Grey out of the Army; but at the moment he did not attach importance to it. It was the kind of threat that an angry man would be pretty sure to make in the circumstances.

Having dismissed Elizabeth Twitcher, he came to lunch with the impression strong on him that he had made as much progress as could be expected in one morning towards the solution of the problem. He was quite undecided whether Hutchings' presence in the Castle at so late an hour, and the probability that he had entered and left it by the library window, or the matter of the woman who had had the stormy interview with the murdered man, was the more important. It must be his early task to discover who that woman was.

He found Mr. Manley awaiting him in the little dining-room, ready to play host. Over their soup and fish they talked about ordinary topics and a little about themselves. Mr. Manley learned that Mr. Flexen had been in the Indian Police for over seven years, and had been forced to resign his post by the breaking down of his health; that during the war he had twice acted as Chief Constable and three times as stipendiary magistrate in different districts. Mr. Flexen gathered that Mr. Manley had fought in France with a brilliant intrepidity which had not met with the public recognition it deserved, and learned that he had been invalided out of the Army owing to the weakness of his heart. This common failure of health was a bond of sympathy between them, and made them well disposed to one another.

There came a pause in this personal talk, and either of them addressed himself to the consumption of the wing of a chicken with a certain absorption in the occupation. It was not uncharacteristic of Mr. Manley that his high sense of the fitness of things had not prevailed on him to accord the liver wing to the guest. He was firmly eating it himself.

Then Mr. Flexen said: "I suppose you came across Hutchings, the butler, pretty often. What kind of a fellow was he?"

"He was rather more like his master than if he had been his twin brother, except that he wore whiskers and not a beard," said Mr. Manley, in a tone of hearty dislike.

"He does not appear to have been at all popular with the other servants," said Mr. Flexen.

"He certainly wasn't popular with me," said Mr. Manley dryly.

"What did Lord Loudwater discharge him for?"

"A matter of a commission on the purchase of some wine," said Mr. Manley. Then in a more earnest tone he added: "Look here: the trenches knock a good deal of the nonsense out of one, and I tell you frankly that if I could help you in any way to discover the criminal, I wouldn't. My feeling is that if ever anyone wanted putting out of the way, Lord Loudwater did; and as he was put out of the way quite painlessly, probably it was a valuble action, whatever its motive."

"I expect that a good many people have come back from the trenches with very different ideas about justice," said Mr. Flexen in an indulgent tone. "The Indian Police also changes your ideas about it. But it's my duty to see that justice is done, and I shall. Besides, I'm very keen on solving this problem, if I can. It seems that Hutchings was in the Castle last night about eleven o'clock, and as you said something about coming down for a drink about that time, I thought you might possibly know something about his movements."

"Well, as it happens," said Mr. Manley and stopped short, paused, and went on: "You seem to have made up your mind that it was a murder and not a suicide."

"So you do know something about the movements of Hutchings," said Mr. Flexen, smiling. "You'll be subpoenaed, you know, if he is charged with the murder."

"That would, of course, be quite a different matter," said Mr. Manley gravely.

"As to its being a murder, I've pretty well made up my mind that it was," said Mr. Flexen.

Mr. Manley looked at him gravely: "You have, have you?" he said. Then he added: "About that knife and the finger-prints on it, if it happens to have recorded any: I've been thinking that you may find yourself suffering from an embarrassment of riches. I know that mine will be on it, and Lady Loudwater's, who used it to cut the leaves of a volume of poetry the day before yesterday, and Hutchings', who cut the string of a parcel of books with it yesterday, and very likely the fingerprints of Lord Loudwater. You know how it is with a knife like that, which lies open and handy. Everyone uses it. I've seen Lady Loudwater use it to cut flowers, and Lord Loudwater to cut the end off a cigar–cursing, of course, because he couldn't lay his hands on a cigar-cutter, and the knife was blunt–and I've cut all kinds of things with it myself."

"Yes; but the finger-prints of the murderer, if it does record them, will be on the top of all those others. I shall simply take prints from all of you and eliminate them."

"Of course; you can get at it that way," said Mr. Manley.

They were silent while Holloway set the cheese-straws on the table.

When he had left the room Mr. Flexen said in a casual tone: "You don't happen to know whether Lord Loudwater was mixed up with any woman in the neighbourhood?"

Mr. Manley paused, then laughed and said: "It's no use at all. When I told you that I would throw no light on the matter, if I could help it, I really meant it. At the same time, I don't mind saying that, with his reputation for brutality, I should think it very unlikely."

"You can never tell about women. So many of them seem to prefer brutes. And, after all, a peer is a peer," said Mr. Flexen.

"There is that," said Mr. Manley in thoughtful agreement.

But he was frowning faintly as he cudgelled his brains in the effort to think what had set Mr. Flexen on the track of Helena Truslove, for it must be Helena.

"I expect I shall be able to find out from his lawyers," said Mr. Flexen.

"This promises to be interesting–the intervention of Romance," said Mr. Manley in a tone of livelier interest. "I took it that the murder, if it was a murder, would be a sordid business, in keeping with Lord Loudwater himself. But if you're going to introduce a lady into the case, it promises to be more fruitful in interest for the dramatist. I'm writing plays."

But Mr. Flexen was not going to divulge the curious fact that about the time of his murder Lord Loudwater had had a violent quarrel with a lady. He had no doubt that Mrs. Carruthers would keep it to herself.

"Oh, one has to look out forevery possible factor in a problem like this, you know," he said carelessly.

The faint frown lingered on Mr. Manley's brow. Mr. Flexen supposed that it was the result of his refraining from gratifying his appetite for the dramatic. They were silent a while.

"When are you going to take our finger-prints?" said Mr. Manley presently.

"Not till I've learned whether there are any on the handle of the knife," said Mr. Flexen. "Perkins has already sent it off to Scotland Yard."

"I never thought of that. It would be rather a waste of time to take them before knowing that," said Mr. Manley.

Holloway brought the coffee; Mr. Manley gave Mr. Flexen an excellent cigar, and they talked about the war. Mr. Flexen drank his coffee quickly, said that he must get back to his work, and added that he hoped that he would enjoy the company of Mr. Manley at dinner. Mr. Manley had been going to dine with Helena Truslove; but after Mr. Flexen's question whether Lord Loudwater had been entangled with any woman in the neighbourhood, he thought that he had better dine with him. He might learn something useful, if he could induce Mr. Flexen to expand under the relaxing influence of dinner. He resolved to use his authority to have the most engaging wine the cellar held. He was determined to make every endeavour to keep Helena's name out of the affair, and he thought that he would succeed.

Mr. Flexen left him. He finished his coffee, the second cup, slowly, wondering about Mr. Flexen's question about Lord Loudwater and a woman. Then, since he had done all the work he could think of, in the way of making arrangements for the funeral, during the morning, he set out briskly to Helena's house, hoping that she would be able to throw some light on it.

He greeted her with his usual warmth, and then, when he came to look at her at his leisure, it was plain to him that the murder had been a much greater shock to her than he had expected. He was surprised at it, for she had assured him that she had never been really in love with Lord Loudwater, and he had believed her. But there was no doubt that she had been greatly upset by the news of his death. Her high colouring was dimmed; she wore a harassed air, and she was uncommonly nervous and ill at ease. He thought it strange that she should be so deeply affected by the death of a man she had such good reason to detest. But, of course, there was no telling how a woman would take anything; Lady Loudwater's distress had fallen as far short of what he had expected as Helena's had exceeded it.

To Mr. Manley's credit it must be admitted that in less than twenty minutes Helena Truslove was looking another creature; her face had recovered all its colour; the harassed air had vanished from it, and she was sitting on his knee in a condition of the most pleasant repose. It was his theory that a woman was never too ill, or too ill at ease, or too unhappy to be made love to. He had acted on it.

When he had thus restored her peace of mind, he told her that Mr. Flexen had asked him whether the late Lord Loudwater had been mixed up with any lady in the neighbourhood, and asked her if she could suggest any reason for his having asked the question. She appeared greatly startled to hear of it. But she could not suggest any reason for his having asked the question. He then asked her about the manner in which the allowance had been paid to her, and was pleased to learn that there was little likelihood of Mr. Flexen's learning that she had received such an allowance from Lord Loudwater, for it had been paid her through a young lawyer of the name of Shepherd, at Low Wycombe, the lawyer who had dealt with the matter of the transference of the house they were in to her, from the rents of some houses Lord Loudwater owned in that town, and that lawyer was somewhere in Mesopotamia, his practice in abeyance.

She was in entire accord with Mr. Manley about the advantage of her name not being connected in any way with the tragedy at the Castle. She pointed out that it was also an advantage that she had just, been paid her allowance for the present quarter, and there would not be another payment for three months. By that time it was probable that the murder would have passed out of people's minds and Mr. Flexen be busy with other work. It seemed to Mr. Manley that Mr. Flexen would not easily learn about the allowance unless Mr. Carrington also knew it, which seemed unlikely, though it was always possible that there was some record of it among the Lord Loudwater's papers at the Castle. Soon after seven he left her to walk back to dine with Mr. Flexen.

Mr. Flexen had had a considerable surprise that afternoon. He had told Robert Black to find William Roper and bring him to him. He wished to hear the story he had told Lord Loudwater the evening before, for it might be of a triviality to make the hypothesis that Lord Loudwater had committed suicide yet less worthy of serious consideration. Black was a long while finding William Roper, for he was at work in the woods. Indeed, he had not yet heard that Lord Loudwater had been murdered, for he had been up most of the night, risen late, got his own breakfast in his out-of-the-way cottage in the depths of the West wood, and gone out on his rounds. The constable found him at the cottage, in the act of preparing his dinner, or rather his tea and dinner, at a quarter to four.

William Roper was startled, indeed, to hear of the murder, and then bitterly annoyed. All the while on his rounds he had been congratulating himself on his coming promotion, and reckoning up the many advantages which would accrue from it, not the least of which was a wider prospect of finding a wife. The cup was dashed from his lips. He had acquired no merit in the eyes of the new Lord Loudwater, and he had most probably made the present Lady Loudwater his enemy, if the murdered man had divulged the source of his knowledge of her goings-on with Colonel Grey. He ate his mixed meal very sulkily, listening to the constable's account of the circumstances of the crime. Slowly, however, his face grew brighter as he listened; the new information he had obtained for his murdered employer might very well have an important bearing on the crime itself. He might yet establish himself as the benefactor of the family.

On the way to the Castle he was so mysterious with Robert Black that the stout constable became a prey to mingled curiosity and doubt. He could not make up his mind whether William Roper really knew something of importance or was merely vapouring. William Roper neither gratified his curiosity, nor banished his doubt. He was alive to the advantage of reserving his information for the most important ear, so as to gain the greatest possible credit for it.

At the first sight of him Mr. Flexen felt that he had before him an important witness, for he took a violent dislike to him, and he had observed, in the course of his many years' experience in the detection of crime, that the most important witness in hounding down a criminal was very often of a repulsive type, the nark type. William Roper was of that type, but his story was indeed startling.

He first told how he had seen Colonel Grey kiss Lady Loudwater in the afternoon–Mr. Flexen noted that Lord Loudwater had accused her of kissing Grey–and of their spending most of the afternoon in the pavilion in the East wood. The time of his watching had already lengthened in William Roper's memory. There was nothing new in these facts, and Mr. Flexen saw no reason to suppose that they had any bearing on the crime. But William Roper went on to say that soon after ten in the evening he had been on his round in the East wood, when he saw Colonel Grey walking in the direction of the Castle. His curiosity had been aroused by what he had seen in the afternoon, and thinking it not unlikely that he was on his way to another meeting with the Lady Loudwater, and that it was the duty of a faithful retainer to make sure about it, with a view to informing his master should his surmise prove correct, he followed him.

The Colonel went straight through the wood into the Castle garden, walked round the Castle, keeping in its shadow as he went, till he stood under the window of Lady Loudwater's suite of rooms.

There he appeared to suffer a check. There was a light in the room on the ground floor under her boudoir. The Colonel had waited quite a while; then he had walked round the Castle and into it by the library window.

William, greatly surprised by the Colonel's audacity, had taken up his position in a clump of tall rhododendrons, opposite the library window, from which he could keep watch on it.

"What time would this be?" said Mr. Flexen.

"It couldn't have been more than twenty minutes past ten, sir," said William Roper.

"And what happened then?" said Mr. Flexen.

"Nothing 'appened for a good ten minutes. Then James Hutchings, the butler, come across the gardens from the south gate, as if 'e'd come from the village, and 'e went in through the libery winder–the same winder."

Mr. Flexen had thought it not unlikely that Hatchings had entered the Castle by that entrance. He was pleased to have his guess corroborated.

"That would be about half-past ten," he said. "Could you see into the library at all?"

"Only a very little way, sir."

"You couldn't see whether Colonel Grey and then James Hutchings went straight through it into the hall, or whether either of them went into the smoking-room?"

"No; I couldn't see so far in as that, though there was a light burning in the libery," said William Roper.

That was a new fact. Anyone passing through the library would be able to see the open knife lying in the big inkstand.

"Go on," said Mr. Flexen. "What happened next?"

"Nothing 'appened for a long while–twenty minutes, I should think–and then there come a woman round the right-'and corner of the Castle wall and along it and into the libery winder. At first I thought it was Mrs. Carruthers, or one of the maids–she were too tall for her ladyship–but it warn't."

"Are you quite sure?" said Mr. Flexen.

"Quite, sir. I should have known 'er if she had been. Besides, she was all muffled up like. You couldn't see 'er face."

"Did she hesitate before going through the library window?" said Mr. Flexen.

"Not as I noticed. She seemed to go straight in."

"As if she were used to going into the Castle that way?" said Mr. Flexen.

William Roper scratched his head. Then he said cautiously: "She seemed to know that way in all right, sir."

"And how was she dressed?" said Mr. Flexen.

"She wasn't in black. It wasn't as dull as black, but it was dullish. It might have been grey and again it might not. It might have been blue or brown. You see, there was a fair moon, sir, but it was be'ind the Castle, an' I never seed 'er in the full moonlight, as you may say, seeing as, coming and going, she come along the wall and went round the right 'and corner of it, in the shadder."

"And which of these three people came away first?" said Mr. Flexen.

"She did. She wasn't in the Castle more nor twenty minutes—if that."

"Did she seem to be in a hurry when she came out? Did she run, or walk quickly?"

"No. I can't say as she did. She went away just about as she came—in no purtic'ler 'urry," said William Roper.

Mr. Flexen paused, considering; then he said: "And who was the next to leave?"

"The Colonel, 'e come out next—in about ten minutes."

"Did he seem in a hurry?"

"'E walked pretty brisk, and 'e was frowning, like as if 'e was in a rage. 'E passed me close, so I 'ad a good look at 'im. Yes; I should say 'e was fair boilen', 'e was," said William Roper, in a solemn, pleased tone of one giving damning evidence.

Mr. Flexen did not press the matter. He said: "So James Hutchings came away last?"

"Yes; about five minutes after the Colonel. And 'e was in a pretty fair to-do, too. Leastways, he was frowning and a-muttering of to 'imself. He passed me close."

"Did *he* seem in any hurry?" said Mr. Flexen.

"'E was walkin' fairly fast," said William Roper.

Mr. Flexen paused again, pondering. He thought that William Roper had thrown all the light on the matter he could; and he had certainly revealed a number of facts which looked uncommonly important.

"And that was all you saw?" he said.

"That was all–except 'er ladyship," said William Roper.

"Her ladyship?" said Mr. Flexen sharply.

"Yes. You see, there was no 'urry for me to go back to the woods, sir; an' I sat down on one of them garden seats along the edge of the Wellin'tonia shrubbery to smoke a pipe and think it ou'. I felt it was my dooty like to let 'is lordship know about these goings-on, never thinking as 'ow 'e was sitting there all the time with a knife in 'im. I should think it was twenty minutes arter that I saw 'er ladyship come out. Of course, I was farther away from the window, but I saw 'er quite plain."

"And where did she go?" said Mr. Flexen.

"She didn't go nowhere, so to speak. She just walked up an' down the gravel path–like as if she'd come out for a breath of fresh air. Then she went in. She wasn't out more nor ten minutes, or a quarter of an hour."

Mr. Flexen was silent in frowning thought; then he looked earnestly at William Roper for a good minute; then he said: "Well, this may be important, or it may not. But it is very important that you should keep it to yourself." He looked hard again at William, decided that an appeal to his vanity would be best, and added: "You're pretty shrewd, I fancy, and you can see that it is most important not to put the criminal on his guard–if it was a crime."

"I suppose I shall 'ave to tell what I know at the inquest?" said William Roper, with an air of importance.

Mr. Flexen gazed at him thoughtfully, weighing the matter. Here were a number of facts which might or might not have an important bearing on the murder, but which would give rise to a great deal of painful and harmful scandal if they were given to the world at this juncture.

Besides the publication of them might force his hand, and he preferred to have a free hand in this matter as he had been used to have a free hand in India. There he had dealt with more than one case in such a manner as to secure substantial justice rather than the exact execution of the law. It might be that in this case justice would be best secured by leaving the murderer to his, or her, conscience rather than by causing several people great unhappiness by bringing about a conviction. He was inclined to think, with Mr. Manley, that the murderer might have performed a public service by removing Lord Loudwater from the world he had so ill adorned. At any rate, he was resolved to have a free hand to deal with the case, and most certainly he was not going to allow this noxious young fellow to hamper his freedom of action and final decision.

"Your evidence seems to me of much too great importance to be given at the inquest. It must be reserved for the trial," he said in an impressive tone. "But if it gets abroad that you have seen what you have told me, the criminal will be prepared to upset your evidence; and it will probably become quite worthless. You must not breathe a word about what you saw to a soul till we have your evidence supported beyond all possibility of its being refuted. Do you understand?"

For a moment William Roper looked disappointed. He had looked to become famous that very day. But he realized his great importance in the affair, and his face cleared.

"I understands, sir," he said with a dark solemnity.

"Not a word," said Mr. Flexen yet more impressively.

8

That morning Olivia went to meet Grey in a mood very different from that of the afternoon before. Then she had moved on light feet, in high spirits, expectant, even excited. She had not known what was coming, but the prospect had been full of possibilities; and, thanks to the sudden appearance of the cat Melchisidec at the crucial moment, she had not been disappointed. Today she would have gone to meet the man who loved her in yet higher spirits, for there is no blinking the fact that she was wholly unable to grieve for her husband. He had with such thoroughness extirpated the girlish fondness she had felt for him when she married him, that she could not without hypocrisy make even a show of grieving for him. His death had merely removed the barrier between her and the man she loved.

But today she did not go to her tryst in spirits higher for the removal of that barrier. She went more slowly, on heavier, lingering feet. Her eyes were downcast, and her forehead was furrowed by an anxious, brooding frown.

The sight of Colonel Grey, waiting for her at the door of the Pavilion, smoothed the furrows from her forehead and quickened her steps. When the door closed behind them he caught her in his arms and kissed her. It was early in her widowhood to be kissed, but she made no protest. She did not feel a widow; she felt a free woman again. It is even to be feared that her lips were responsive.

Antony, too, was changed. He was paler and almost careworn. There was no doubt of his joy at her coming, no doubt that it was greater than the day before. But it was qualified by some other troubling emotion. Now and again he looked at her with different eyes–eyes from

which the joy had of a sudden faded, rather fearful eyes
that looked a question which could not be asked. Her eyes
rather shrank from his, and when they did look into them
it was with a like question.

But they were too deeply in love with one another for
any other emotion to hold them for long at a time.
Presently in the joy of being together, looking at one
another, touching one another, the fearfulness and the
question passed from their eyes.

There was nothing rustic about the Pavilion inside or
out. It was of white marble, brought from Carrara for the
fifth Baron Loudwater at the end of the eighteenth
century; and a whim of her murdered husband had led
him to replace the original, delicate, rather severe
furniture by a most comfortable broad couch, two no less
comfortable chairs with arms, a small red lacquer table
and a dozen cushions. He had hung on each wall a
drawing of dancing-girls by Degas. Since the coverings of
the couch and the cushions were of Chinese silken
embroideries, the interior appeared a somewhat bizarre
mixture of the Oriental and the French.

Antony had been in some doubt that Olivia would
come. But he had thought it natural that she should come
to him in such an hour of distress, for he knew the simple
directness of her nature. Therefore he had taken no
chance. He had gone to High Wycombe, ransacked its
simple provision shops, and brought away a lunch basket.

She was for returning to the Castle to lunch. But he
persuaded her to stay. She needed no great pressing; she
had a feeling that every hour was precious, that it was
unsafe to lose a single one of them: a foreboding that she
and Antony might not be together long. It almost seemed
that a like foreboding weighed on him. At times they
seemed almost feverish in their desire to wring the last
drop of sweetness out of the swiftly flying hour.

After lunch again the thought came to her that she
ought to go back to the Castle, that she might be needed,
and missed; but it found no expression. She could not tear

herself away. She had been denied joy too long, and it was intoxicating.

It was five o'clock before she left the Pavilion. She walked briskly, with her wonted, easy, swinging gait, back to the Castle, in a dream, her anxiety and fear for the while forgotten. On her way up to her suite of rooms she met no one. She was quick to take off her hat and ring for her tea. Elizabeth Twitcher brought it to her, and from her Olivia learned that only Mr. Manley had asked for her. She realized that, after all, thanks to her dead husband, she was but an inconspicuous person in the Castle. No one had been used to consult her in any matter. She was glad of it. At the moment all she desired was freedom of action, freedom to be with Antony; and the fact that the life of the Castle moved smoothly along in the capable hands of Mrs. Carruthers and Mr. Manley gave her that freedom.

After her tea she went out into the rose-garden and was strolling up and down it when Mr. Flexen, pondering the information which he had obtained from William Roper, saw her and came out to her. He thought that she shrank a little at the sight of him, but assured himself that it must be fancy; surely there could be no reason why she should shrink from him.

"I'm told, Lady Loudwater, that you went out through the library window into the garden for a stroll about a quarter to twelve last night. Did you by any chance, as you went in or came out, hear Lord Loudwater snore? I want to fix the latest hour at which he was certainly alive. You see how important it may prove."

She hesitated, wrinkling her brow as she weighed the importance of her answer. Then she looked at him with limpid eyes and said:

"Yes."

He knew—the sixth sense of the criminal investigator told him—that she lied, and he was taken aback. Why should she lie? What did she know? What had she to hide?

"Did you hear him snore going out, or coming in?" he said.

"Both," said Olivia firmly.

Mr. Flexen hesitated. He did not believe her. Then he said: "How long did Lord Loudwater sleep after dinner as a rule? What time did he go to bed?"

"It varied a good deal. Generally he awoke and went to bed before twelve. But sometimes it was nearer one, especially if he was disturbed and went to sleep again."

"Thank you," said Mr. Flexen, and he left her and went back into the Castle.

Lord Loudwater had certainly been disturbed by the woman with whom he had quarrelled. He might have slept on late. But why had Lady Loudwater lied about the snoring? What did she know? What on earth was she hiding? Whom was she screening? Could it be Colonel Grey? Was he mixed up in the actual murder? Mr. Flexen decided that he must have more information about Colonel Grey, that he would get into touch with him, and that soon.

He had information about him sooner than he expected and without seeking it. Inspector Perkins was awaiting him, with Mrs. Turnbull, the landlady of the "Cart and Horses." The inspector had learned from her that the Lord Loudwater had paid a visit to her lodger the evening before, and that they had quarrelled fiercely. Mr. Flexen heard her story and questioned her. The important point in it seemed to him to be Lord Loudwater's threats to hound Colonel Grey out of the Army.

Mrs. Turnbull left him plenty to ponder. Mr. Manley had told him that the handle of the famous knife would probably provide him with an embarrassment of riches in the way of finger-prints. It seemed to him that the stories of William Roper, Mrs. Carruthers, and Mrs. Turnbull had provided him with an embarrassment of riches in the way of possible murderers. It grew clearer than ever to him that the inquest must be conducted with the greatest discretion, that as few facts as possible must be revealed at it. It was also clear to him that, unless the handle of the knife told a plain story, he would get nothing but circumstantial evidence, and so far he had gotten too much of it.

He made up his mind that it would be best to see Colonel Grey at once and form his impression as to the likelihood of his having had a hand in the crime. He was loth to believe that a V.C. would murder in cold blood even as detestable a bully as the Lord Loudwater appeared to have been. But he had seen stranger things. Moreover, it depended on the type of V.C. Colonel Grey was. V.C.s varied.

Mr. Flexen lost no time. It was nearly six o'clock. It was likely that the Colonel would be back at his inn after his fishing. Mrs. Turnbull was sure that he had as usual gone fishing, for, when he set out in the morning, he had taken his rod with him. Antony Grey was not the man to omit a simple precaution like that. Therefore, Mr. Flexen ordered a car to be brought round, and was at the "Cart and Horses" by twenty past six.

He found that Colonel Grey had indeed returned. He sent up his card; the maid came back and at once took him up to the Colonel's sitting-room. Grey received him with an air of inquiry, which grew yet more inquiring when Mr. Flexen told him that he was engaged in investigating the affair of Lord Loudwater's death. Therefore, Mr. Flexen came to the point at once.

"I have been informed that Lord Loudwater paid you a visit last night, and that a violent quarrel ensued, Colonel Grey," he said.

"Pardon me; but the violence was all on Lord Loudwater's part," said Colonel Grey in an exceedingly unpleasant tone. "I merely made myself nasty in a quiet way. Violence is not in my line, unless I'm absolutely driven to it; and anyone less likely to drive anyone to violence than that obnoxious and noisy jackass I've never come across. The fellow was all words–abusive words. He'd no fight in him. I gave him every reason I could think of to go for me because I particularly wanted to hammer him. But he hadn't got it in him."

Grey spoke quietly, without raising his voice, but there was a rasp in his tone that impressed Mr. Flexen. If a man could give such an impression of dangerousness with his voice, what would he be like in action? He realized that here was a quite uncommon type of V. C. He realized, too, that Lord Loudwater had made the mistake of a lifetime in his attempt to bully him. Moreover, he had a strong feeling that if it had seemed to Colonel Grey that Lord Loudwater was better out of the way, and a favourable opportunity had presented itself, he might very well have displayed little hesitation in putting him out of the way. He felt that the obnoxious peer would have been little more than a dangerous dog to him.

He did not speak at once. He looked into Colonel Grey's grey eyes, and cold and hard they were, weighing him. Then he said: "Lord Loudwater threatened to hound you out of the Army, I'm told."

"Among other things," said Grey carelessly.

Mr. Flexen guessed that the other things were threats to divorce Lady Loudwater.

"That would have been a very serious blow to you," he said.

"You're quite–right," said Colonel Grey.

Mr. Flexen could have sworn that he had started to say: "You're quite wrong," and changed his mind.

The Colonel seemed to hesitate for words; then he went on: "It would have been a very heavy blow indeed. You can see that for a man who enlisted in the Artists' Rifles in 1914, and fought his way up to the command of a regiment, nothing could be more painful. It would have been heartbreaking; I should have been years getting over it."

The rasp had gone out of his voice. He was speaking in a pleasant, confidential tone, and Mr. Flexen did not believe a word he said. At the least he was exaggerating the distress he would have felt at leaving the Army; but Mr. Flexen had the strongest feeling that he would have felt next to no distress at all. Again he was astonished. Colonel Grey was lying to him just as Lady Loudwater had lied. What could be their reason? What on earth had they done?

He kept his astonishment out of his face, and said in a sympathetic voice: "Yes, I can see that. And then, again, it would have been painful and very unpleasant to feel that your thoughtlessness had landed Lady Loudwater in the Divorce Court."

"Oh, Lord, no!" said Colonel Grey quickly. "There was no chance of any divorce proceedings. Even for a divorce case, at any rate one brought by the husband, there must be *some* grounds; he must have *some* evidence. The cock-and-bull story of a gamekeeper is hardly enough to found a divorce case on, is it?"

"Oh, I don't know. The gamekeeper might convince a jury. You know what juries are. You can never tell what form their stupidity will take," said Mr. Flexen.

"But apart from the lack of evidence, there was no chance of a divorce case. I tell you, Loudwater hadn't got it in him," said Grey confidently. "He'd have threatened and been abusive. He'd have gone on throwing that cock-and-bull story at Lady Loudwater for as long as she continued to stick to him; but it would have stopped at that. His infernal temper never went any deeper than his lungs. Lady Loudwater had nothing to fear."

"Yet you think that he would have done his best to hound you out of the Army?" said Mr. Flexen, finding this conception of Lord Loudwater as a harmless, if violent, vapourer somewhat inconsistent.

"That's quite another matter," said Grey quickly. "It merely meant using his influence behind my back with some scurvy politician. There wouldn't have been any publicity attached to that, any exposure of his bullying. He'd have done that all right."

"I should have thought that a man of Lord Loudwater's violent temper would rather have sought an open row," Mr. Flexen persisted.

"Of course—if he'd been really violent. But he wasn't, I tell you. He was only a blustering bully where women and servants were concerned—people he could cow. I tell you, I made it quite clear that he crumpled up directly you stood up to him. Why, hang it all! Any man with the soul of a mouse who really believed that I had been making love to his wife, couldn't have taken the things I told him without going for me at any risk. And as I'm still rather crocked up, and he knew it, there must have seemed precious little risk about it. I tell you that he was just a blustering ruffian."

Mr. Flexen had a strong impression that Colonel Grey was unused to being as expansive as this, that he was talking for talking's sake, possibly to put him off asking some question which would be difficult or dangerous to answer. He could not for the life of him think what that question could be.

"I daresay you're right," he said carelessly. "Bullies aren't over-fond of a real scrap. But I am told that you paid a visit to the Castle last night and came away about a quarter past eleven. Did you?"

Colonel Grey showed no faintest disquiet on hearing that his visit to Olivia the night before was known. But he did not give Mr. Flexen time to finish the sentence.

He interrupted him, saying quickly: "Yes. I went to see Lady Loudwater. I thought it likely that she would attach a good deal more importance to Loudwater's silly threats than they deserved and might be worrying. It would have been quite natural. I wanted to talk it over with her and set her mind at rest about it. It didn't take very long to do that, partly because it was a long time since he had really frightened her. She had got used to his tantrums and bullying; and even this new game had not disturbed her very much. We both came to the conclusion that he was just blustering again, and wouldn't do anything. As a matter of fact, I don't think she cared very much what he did. She had got so fed up with him that she didn't care whether they separated or not."

Mr. Flexen felt more sure than ever that this garrulity was unusual in Colonel Grey. He was talking with a purpose, apparently to induce him to believe that both he and Lady Loudwater had taken her husband's threat of divorce proceedings lightly. He began to think that they had not taken it lightly at all, or, at any rate, one or other of them had not.

"Yes," he said. "That's what always happens with those blustering' fellows. In the end no one takes them seriously. But what I came to ask you was: Did you, as you came through the library or went out through it, hear Lord Loudwater snore?"

Colonel Grey hesitated, just as Lady Loudwater had hesitated over that question. Plainly he was weighing the effect of his answer.

Then he said: "No."

Mr. Flexen's instinct assured him that Colonel Grey had lied just as Lady Loudwater had lied.

"Are you sure that nothing in the nature of a snore came to your ears as you came out? Did you hear any sound from the room? You can see how important it is to fix as near as we possibly can the hour of Lord Loudwater's death," he said earnestly.

"No, I heard nothing," said Colonel Grey firmly.

"Bother!" said Mr. Flexen. "It's very important. Possibly I shall be able to find out from someone else."

"I hope you will," said Grey politely.

Mr. Flexen bade him good-night cordially enough, and drove back to the Castle in a considerable perplexity.

Both Colonel Grey and Lady Loudwater were behaving in an uncommonly odd, not to say suspicious manner.

He was quite sure that both of them had lied about the dead man's snoring. But it was plain that either had lied with a different object. Lady Loudwater had lied to make it appear that her husband had been alive at midnight. Colonel Grey had lied to make it appear that he was dead at a quarter-past eleven. But Mr. Flexen was sure that Colonel Grey had heard Lord Loudwater snore and that Lady Loudwater had not.

What did they know? What had they done? Or what had one of them done?

9

When Mr. Flexen reached the Castle Wilkins took him to a bedroom in the west wing. He found that his portmanteau had arrived, had been unpacked, and that his dress clothes were laid out ready for him on the bed.

As he dressed he cudgelled his brains for the reason why Lady Loudwater and Colonel Grey had lied. Then an idea came to him: were they lying to shield the unknown woman with whom Lord Loudwater had had that violent quarrel? The longer he considered this hypothesis the more possible it grew.

He must find that unknown woman, and at once. Possibly Mr. Carrington, as Lord Loudwater's legal adviser, would be able to put him on her track.

He came to dinner, still perplexed, to find Mr. Manley waiting to bear him company. They talked for a while about public affairs and the weather.

Then Mr. Flexen said: "Was Lord Loudwater the kind of man to confide in his lawyers?"

"Not if he could help it," said Mr. Manley with conviction.

Mr. Flexen hoped that Lord Loudwater had not been able to help confiding in his lawyers about this unknown woman.

Then he said: "By the way, do you know Colonel Grey?"

"Oh, yes. He was here a lot up to a little while ago. Then he had a row, the inevitable row, with Lord Loudwater, and he hasn't been here since. He dropped on to Lord Loudwater for bullying Lady Loudwater, and he didn't drop on him lightly either. Hell, I fancy, was what he gave him."

"Yes; I gathered that something of the kind had taken place. What kind of a man is the Colonel?" said Mr. Flexen carelessly.

"The best man in the world not to have a row with. He's a cold terror," said Mr. Manley, in a tone of enthusiastic conviction. "He always seems rather cooler than a cucumber. But my belief is that that coolness is just the mask of really violent emotions. I saw them working once. I came in on the end of his row with Loudwater–just the end of it–my goodness! From my point of view, the dramatist's, you know, he's the most interesting person in the county–bar Lady Loudwater, of course."

"I should never have thought him a terror," said Mr. Flexen, in a tone of somewhat incredulous surprise. "I had a talk with him this evening about Lord Loudwater's death, and he seemed to me to be a pleasant enough fellow and an excellent soldier. I take it that he's very keen on his career in the Army?"

"Not a bit of it. The war is merely a side issue with him," said Mr. Manley in an assured tone. "I know from what he told me himself. We were talking over our experiences."

"But, hang it all! He's a V. C.!" cried Mr. Flexen.

"Yes, he's a V. C. all right. But that's because he's one of those men who have the knack of taking an interest in everything they turn their hands to, and doing it well. But his two passions are Chinese art and women," said Mr. Manley.

"Women?" said Mr. Flexen. "He didn't strike me as being that kind of man at all. He seemed a quite simple, straightforward soldier."

"Simplicity and a passion for Chinese art don't go together–at least, not what is usually called simplicity," said Mr. Manley dryly. "A friend of mine, who knows all about him, told me that he had had more really serious love affairs than any other man in London. He seems to be one of those men who fall in love hard every time they fall in love. He said that it was one of the mysteries of the polite world how he had kept out of the Divorce Court."

"Sounds an odd type," said Mr. Flexen, storing up the information, and marking how little it agreed with his own observation of Colonel Grey. "And you say that Lady Loudwater is interesting too?"

"Oh, come! Are you pumping me or merely pulling my leg?" said Mr. Manley. "Surely you can see that Lady Loudwater is pure Italian Renaissance. She is one of those subtle, mysterious creatures that Leonardo and Luini were always painting, compact of emotion."

"It's so long since I was at Balliol, and then I was doing Indian Civil work—the languages, you know. I've forgotten all I knew about the Renaissance in Italy, and I don't look at many pictures. All the same, I think you're wrong—your dramatic imagination, you know. My own idea is that Lady Loudwater, at any rate, is a quite simple creature."

"It isn't mine," said Mr. Manley firmly. "She's a great deal too intelligent to be simple, and she comes of far too intelligent a family."

"What family?" said Mr. Flexen.

"She's a Quainton, with Italian blood in her veins."

"The deuce she is!" cried Mr. Flexen, and half a dozen stories of the Quaintons rose in his mind.

He must amend his impressions of Lady Loudwater.

"And she has a keener sense of humour than any woman I ever came across," said Mr. Manley, driving his contention home.

"Has she?" said Mr. Flexen.

There was a pause. Then Mr. Manley said in a musing tone: "Do you suppose that Colonel Grey finds her simple?"

"What? You don't think that there is really anything serious between them?" said Mr. Flexen quickly.

"No, not really serious—at any rate, on Colonel Grey's part. You can hardly expect a man, recovering very slowly from three bad wounds and still crocked up, to fall in love, can you? Especially a man who, when he does fall in love, falls in love with the violence with which Grey is charged," said Mr. Manley.

"There is that," said Mr. Flexen. "But that wouldn't prevent Lady Loudwater from falling in love with Colonel Grey. And after the way her husband treated her, she must have needed something in the way of affection—badly."

"It's no good a woman falling in love with a man unless he falls in love with her," said Mr. Manley, in the tone of a philosopher. "Besides, women don't fall in love with men who are so feeble from illness as the Colonel seems to be. How can there be the attraction? She might, of course, want to mother him very keenly. But that's quite a different thing." He paused, then added in a tone of some anxiety: "I say, you're not trying to mix her up with the murder—if it was a murder?"

"I'm not trying to mix anybody up in it," said Mr. Flexen slowly. "But I don't mind telling you that it is growing quite a pretty problem, and to solve a problem you must have every factor in it. You see that the strong point about both Lady Loudwater and Colonel Grey is, on your own showing, that they are uncommonly clever; and only stupid people commit murder—except, of course, once in a blue moon."

"But what about these gangs of criminals we sometimes read about, with extraordinarily clever men at the head of them? Don't they exist?" said Mr. Manley, in a tone of surprise.

"They exist; but they don't commit murders—not in Europe, at any rate," said Mr. Flexen. "In the East and in the United States it's different perhaps. Murder is always as much of a blunder as a crime. It makes people so keen after the criminal. No: no really intelligent criminal commits murder."

"Of course, that's true," said Mr. Manley readily. He paused, then added in a thoughtful tone: "I wonder whether the war has weakened our conception of the sanctity of human life?"

"I shouldn't wonder," said Mr. Flexen; and their talk drifted into a discussion of generalities.

He was glad that he was staying at the Castle. His talk with Mr. Manley had been illuminating.

Olivia dined in her sitting-room, and with a poor appetite. Away from Grey, she had fallen back into her anxiety and fearfulness. Wilkins was waiting on her, an insensible block of a fellow; but even he perceived that she was very little aware of what she was eating, and now and again paused, and in some worrying train of thought forgot that she was dining at all.

After dinner, however, her mood changed. The fearfulness and anxiety at times vanished from her face, and a pleasant, eager expectancy took their place.

At a quarter to nine she took a dark wrap from her wardrobe, went quietly down the stairs, and slipped out of the side door, across the east lawn, and into the path through the shrubbery, unseen. Grey had suggested that he should come to the Castle after dinner to spend the evening with her; but they had decided that it would be wiser to meet in the pavilion. There would be talk if he spent the evening with her so soon after her husband's death, with his body still unburied in the house. This was the only mention they made of him all the time they spent together. Besides, both of them found the pavilion in the wood a far more delightful meeting-place than the Castle. In the pavilion they felt that they were out of the world.

Grey, too anxious and restless to await her at the pavilion, had come down the wood and into the end of the path through the shrubbery. It startled her to come upon him so suddenly. But when they came out of the shrubbery into the moonlit aisle of the wood, the fearfulness and anxiety and restlessness had vanished utterly from their faces; both of them were smiling.

They walked slowly, saying little, touching now and again as they swayed in their walk along the turf. It seemed wiser not to light the candles in the pavilion. The moonlight, shining through the high windows, gave them light enough to see one another's eyes. It was all they needed. The time passed quickly in the ineffable confidences of lovers. They had a hundred things to tell one another, a hundred things to ask one another, in their effort to attain that oneness which is the aim of all true love. But in their joy in being together, in the joy of both of them, there was a feverishness, a sense that it was a menaced joy which must needs be brief. Again they were striving to wring the most out of the hour which was so swiftly passing. At times the sense of danger which hung over them was so strong, that they clung to one another like frightened children in the dark.

Though Mr. Flexen had at the time shown himself somewhat unbelieving in the matter of Mr. Manley's conclusions about the character and temperament of Grey and Olivia, the impression they had made on him grew stronger. He was too good a judge of men not to perceive that the budding dramatist had the intelligent imagination which makes for real shrewdness, and he was not disposed to underrate the value of the imagination in forming judgments of men and women. Probably Colonel Grey was a man of less intensity of emotion than Mr. Manley had declared, and Lady Loudwater less subtile and intelligent. But, after making these reductions, he had here possible actors in a drama of passion; and though it was his experience that money, not passion, is the most frequent motive of murder, he must take the probability of Lord Loudwater's murder being a crime of passion into account, though, of course, the violent Hutchings, threatened with ruin, would undoubtedly benefit from a monetary point of view by the murder. At the same time, Hutchings had just had an interview, which had gone better probably than he had expected, with an uncommonly pretty girl.

Mr. Carrington arrived soon after breakfast next morning, and Mr. Flexen at once discussed the matter of the inquest with him and the Coroner. He found the lawyer chiefly eager to have as little scandal as possible, and the Coroner took his cue from the lawyer. This suited Mr. Flexen admirably. He had no wish to show his hand so early. He foresaw that if the story of William Roper were told, and the story of Lord Loudwater's quarrel with Colonel Grey at the "Cart and Horses," there would be a painful scandal. The majority of the people of the neighbourhood would at once believe and declare that Lady Loudwater, or Colonel Grey, or both, had murdered Lord Loudwater. Such a scandal would in no way serve his purpose. It might rather hamper him. Pressure might be put on him which might force him to take steps before the time was ripe for them.

There was no difficulty in their having exactly the kind of inquest they wanted, for it was wholly in the hands of Mr. Flexen and the Coroner. After careful discussion they decided to limit it to Dr. Thornhill's evidence, and that of the servants with regard to the dead nobleman's mood on the night of his death. Mr. Carrington urged strongly that full prominence should be given to the fact that the wound might have been self-inflicted, and the Coroner promised that this should be done.

When the Coroner had left them the lawyer said to Mr. Flexen: "In the case of a man like the late Lord Loudwater, you can't be too careful, you know. Really, it would be better if the jury brought in a verdict of suicide. A suicide in a family is always better than a murder."

"H'm! You could hardly expect me to rest content with such a verdict," said Mr. Flexen. "Not, I mean, on the evidence."

"Oh, no; I shouldn't," said Mr. Carrington. "All I want to avoid is a lot of quite unnecessary painful scandal, which won't lead to anything of use to you, about innocent

people connected with my late client. You won't act
without something pretty definite to go upon, while the
scandalmongers will talk on no grounds at all. Lord
Loudwater was a queer customer, and goodness knows
what will come to light, for, of course, you'll investigate
the affair thoroughly."

The inquest accordingly was conducted on these lines.
Only Dr. Thornhill, Wilkins and Holloway were called as
witnesses; and the Coroner directed the jury to bring in a
verdict to the effect that Lord Loudwater had died of a
knife-wound, and that there was no evidence to show
whether it was self-inflicted or not.

But in this he failed. The jury, muddle-headed,
obstinate country folk, had made up their minds that
Lord Loudwater was the kind of man to be murdered, and
that, therefore, he had been murdered. They brought in
the verdict that Lord Loudwater had been murdered by
some person or persons unknown.

Mr. Flexen, Mr. Carrington and the Coroner were
annoyed, but they had had too wide an experience of
juries to be surprised.

"This will let loose a horde of reporters on us," said
Mr. Carrington very gloomily.

"It will," said Mr. Flexen. "The pet sleuths of the *Wire*
and the *Planet* will leave London in about an hour."

"Well, they'll have to be dealt with," said Mr.
Carrington.

"Oh, they're all right. I probably know them. I'll get
them to work with me. They must be treated very nicely,"
said Mr. Flexen cheerfully.

"They're always a confounded nuisance," said Mr.
Carrington, frowning.

"Not if they're kindly treated. Indeed, I shall very
likely find them really useful," said Mr. Flexen. "But you
might give the servants a hint to be careful of what they
say. The hint will come best from you, and be much more
effective than if it came from anyone else. You represent
the family."

"I'll see about it," said Mr. Carrington, and he went to Olivia's boudoir to confer with her about the invitations to the funeral.

Mr. Flexen was, indeed, little disturbed by the prospect of the coming of the newspaper men. A popular member of the chief literary and journalistic club in London, he would probably know them, or they would know of him; and he would find them ready enough to work with him. Besides, even if they discovered that the quarrel between Colonel Grey and Lord Loudwater had its origin in Lady Loudwater, in the present state of mind of the country, they would have to move very cautiously indeed in the case of a V.C.

He did not, indeed, think it likely that they would discover the cause of the quarrel for some time—possibly not before their papers had tired of the business and sent them on other errands. Mrs. Turnbull only knew of Lord Loudwater's threat to hound Colonel Grey out of the Army; she did not know the reason of his fury and his threat. Elizabeth Twitcher would certainly hold her tongue about Lord Loudwater's subsequent quarrel with Lady Loudwater, and his accusations and threats; Mrs. Carruthers was even more unlikely to tell of it. It was unlikely that William Roper would come within the ken of the newspaper men. No one could tell them that he was the great repository of facts in the case, and Mr. Flexen believed that he had given him good cause to keep his mouth shut till he called on him to open it.

Taking one thing with another, he thought it more than likely that the newspaper men would not hinder him in his purpose of dealing with the affair in his own way.

On the other hand, they might very well be used to help him discover the unknown woman who had had the furious quarrel with Lord Loudwater at about eleven o'clock. Indeed, he regarded the information about that quarrel as a sop to be thrown to them. She afforded just the element of melodrama in the case which would be most grateful to their different newspapers, and provide them with plenty of the kind of headlines which best sold them. It was certain that James Hutchings would also occupy their attention. The fact that he had been discharged with contumely and threats, that he had departed uttering violent threats against the dead man, and that he had returned to visit Elizabeth Twitcher late that night, were doubtless being discussed by the whole neighbourhood. However, only himself and William Roper knew, at present, that James Hutchings had come and gone by the library window, had actually passed twice within a few feet of his sleeping, or dead, master. That fact, also, Mr. Flexen proposed to keep to himself till he saw reason to divulge it. His next business must be to question Hutchings.

It was quite likely that there lay the solution of the mystery.

10

It would have been easy enough for Mr. Flexen to send for Hutchings to the Castle and question him there. But he did not. In the first place, he did not think it fair to a man who had already prejudiced himself so seriously by his threats against the murdered man. Besides, he would be at a disadvantage, under a greater strain at the Castle, and Mr. Flexen wanted him where he would be at his best, for he wished to be able to form an exact judgment of the likelihood of his being the murderer. Indeed, it must be a very careful and exact judgment, for he felt that he was moving in deep waters; that it was a case in which it was possible, even easy, to go hopelessly wrong. Also, he was fully alive to the fact that if threatened men live long, the men who threaten are to blame for it, and that threats such as Hutchings' are the commonest things in the world, and, as a rule, of very little importance. But there was always the chance that Hutchings was the unusual threatener; and, if he were, he had assuredly been in circumstances most favourable to the carrying out of his threats.

Accordingly he learnt from Inspector Perkins the way to the gamekeeper's cottage in the West Wood, where Hutchings was staying with his father, and drove the car to it himself. Hutchings was alone in the cottage, for his father was out on his rounds. He invited Mr. Flexen to come in. Mr. Flexen came in, sat down in an arm-chair, and examined Hutchings' face. He saw that the man was plainly very anxious and ill at ease. It was natural enough. He must perceive quite clearly how black against him things looked.

He was forced also to admit to himself that Hutchings had not a pleasant face. It was choleric and truculent, and in spite of the man's evident anxiety, there was a sullen fierceness on it which gave him no little of the air of a wild beast trapped.

Mr. Flexen wasted no time beating about the bush, but said to him: "When you visited Elizabeth Twitcher last night you entered and left the Castle by the library window."

"You got that from that young blighter Manley," said Hutchings bitterly.

"Not at all. I did not know that Mr. Manley knew it," said Mr. Flexen. "So you did?"

"Yes, sir, I did. I always went to the village that way in the summer-time. It's the shortest. Besides, his lordship was nearly always asleep; and if he wasn't and did 'ear me, there was always something I could be doing in the library, sir."

He spoke with eager, rather humble civility.

"Well, did you, as you went through the library, coming or going, hear Lord Loudwater snore?"

Hutchings knitted his brow, thinking; then he said: "I can't call to mind as I did, sir. But, then, I wasn't giving him any attention. I was thinking about other things altogether. Of course, I went out quietly enough. But that was habit."

"That sounds as if you had not heard him snore—as if you thought that he was awake," said Mr. Flexen.

"I don't think I thought about him at all, sir, at the moment. I was thinking about other things," said Hutchings.

"You say that Mr. Manley saw you go out?"

"Yes, sir. I passed him in the hall and went into the library. We had a few words, and I told him I had come to fetch some cigarettes as I'd left behind."

"Do you know what the time was?" said Mr. Flexen.

"No, sir—not exactly. But it must have been nearly half-past eleven, I should think."

"It is very important to fix the time at which Lord Loudwater died," said Mr. Flexen. "You can't tell me nearer than that?"

"No, sir. It was nearly ten to twelve when I got home, and I reckon it's about twenty minutes' walk from the Castle to the cottage here."

"And all you went to the Castle for was to speak to Elizabeth Twitcher?" said Mr. Flexen.

"That was all I went for—every single thing. And it was all I did there—every mortal thing I did there, sir," Hatchings asseverated, and he wiped his brow.

"H'm!" said Mr. Flexen. "As you passed through the library, did you happen to notice whether the knife was in its place in the big inkstand?"

Hutchings hesitated, and his lips twitched. Then he said: "Yes, I did, sir. It was in the big inkstand."

Mr. Flexen could not make up his mind whether he was telling the truth or not. He thought that he was not. But he did not attach much importance to the matter. People who knew themselves to be suspected of a crime had often told him quite stupid and unnecessary lies and been proved innocent after all.

"I should have thought that your mind was too full of other things to notice a thing like that," he said in a somewhat incredulous tone.

Then there came an outburst. Mr. Flexen had thought that Hutchings was worked up to a high degree of nervous tension, and he was. He cried out that he knew that everyone believed that he had done it; but he hadn't. He'd never thought of it. He was damned if he didn't wish he had done it. He might as well be hung for a sheep as a lamb, anyhow. He broke off to curse Lord Loudwater at length. He had been a curse to everyone who came into contact with him while he was alive, and now he was getting people into trouble when he was dead. Yes: he wished it had occurred to him to stick that knife into him.

He'd have done it like a shot, and he'd have done the right thing. The world was well rid of a swine like that!

His face was contorted, and his eyes kept gleaming red as he talked, and he came to the end of his outburst, trembling and panting.

Mr. Flexen was unmoved and unenlightened. It was merely the outburst of a badly-frightened man lacking in self-control, and told him nothing. It left it equally likely that Hutchings had, or had not, committed the crime.

"There's nothing to get so frantic about," he said quietly to the panting man. "It doesn't do any good."

"It's all very well to talk like that, sir," said Hutchings in a shaky voice. "But I know what people are saying. It's enough to make anyone lose their temper."

"I should think that yours was pretty easy to lose," said Mr. Flexen dryly.

"I know it. It is very short, sir. It always was; and I can't help it," said Hutchings in an apologetic voice.

"Then you'd better set about learning to help it, my man," said Mr. Flexen.

He took out his pipe and filled it slowly. The flush faded a little from Hutchings' face. Mr. Flexen lighted his pipe and rose.

Then as he went to the door he said: "I should advise you to get that stupid temper well in hand. It makes a bad impression. Good afternoon."

Mr. Flexen drove back to the Castle, considering Hutchings carefully. There was no doubt that he was, indeed, badly frightened; but he had reason to be. Mr. Flexen could not decide whether he had worn the air of a guilty man or an innocent. He could not decide whether the butler had been too deeply absorbed in his own affairs to hear the snoring of Lord Loudwater as he went through the library. It was possible that Lord Loudwater was alive, asleep, and yet not snoring at the time. Snoring is often intermittent.

He considered Hutchings' violent outburst. Certainly such an outburst showed the man uncommonly unbalanced; it might, indeed, on occasion take the form of uncontrollable murderous fury. But it seemed to him that an actual meeting with Lord Loudwater would have been necessary to provoke that. But Lord Loudwater had been sitting in his chair when he died; and if he had not killed himself, he had been killed in his sleep. At any rate, there was probably sufficient evidence, seeing what juries are, to convict Hatchings. If he had been one of those not uncommon ministers of the law, whose only desire is to secure a conviction, he would doubtless arrest him at once. But it was not his only desire to secure a conviction; it was his very keen desire to find the right solution of the problem. He could not see where any more evidence against Hutchings was to come from. What Mr. Manley had told him about the knife, that it had been in general use, and that he had seen Hutchings cut string with it the day before the murder, greatly lessened its value as evidence, even if Hutchings' finger-prints were thick on it. He decided to dismiss Hutchings from his mind for the time being, and devote all his energies to discovering the mysterious woman with whom Lord Loudwater had had the furious quarrel between eleven and a quarter-past.

With this end in view, on his return to the Castle, he went straight to the library, where Mr. Carrington was engaged, along with Mr. Manley, in an examination of the murdered man's papers. They were uncommonly few, and Mr. Manley had already set them in order. Lord Loudwater seemed to have kept but few letters, and the papers consisted chiefly of receipted and unreceipted bills.

When he found that Mr. Flexen had come to confer with the lawyer, Mr. Manley assumed an air of extraordinary discretion and softly withdrew.

"I want to know—it is most important—whether there was any entanglement between Lord Loudwater and a woman," said Mr. Flexen.

"I should think it very unlikely," said Mr. Carrington without hesitation. "At least, I have never heard of anything of the kind, and so far I have come across no trace of anything of the kind among his papers."

Mr. Flexen frowned, considering; then he said: "Do you happen to know whether he employed anyone besides your firm to do legal work for him?"

"As to that I can't say. But I should not think it likely. It was always a business to get him to attend to anything that wanted doing, and he always made a fuss about it. I can't see him employing another firm too. But he may have done. The only thing is that I ought to have found either their bills or the receipts for them among those papers—except that my late client does not appear to have taken the trouble to keep many receipts."

"The thing is that I've learnt that Lord Loudwater had a furious quarrel with some unknown woman between eleven and a quarter-past on the night of his death, and I want to find her. You can see how important it is. It may be that she stabbed him, or it may be that she provided him with the motive to commit suicide—not that that seems likely. But you can't tell: she might have been able to threaten him with some exposure. Those people without any self-control are always doing the most senseless things—bigamy, for instance, is often one of their weaknesses."

"Loudwater was certainly without self-control; but I hardly think that he was the man to commit bigamy," said the lawyer.

"It would very much simplify matters if he had," said Mr. Flexen in a dissatisfied tone. "I wonder whether Manley would know anything about it?"

"He might," said Mr. Carrington.

Mr. Flexen went through the library window to find Mr. Manley strolling up and down the lawn with every appearance of enjoying his pipe and the respite from perusing papers.

"Mr. Carrington tells me that you were in Lord Loudwater's confidence," said Mr. Flexen.

"Wholly," said Mr. Manley, with more promptness than his actual knowledge of the facts warranted.

It seemed to him fitting that a secretary of his intelligence and discretion should have been wholly in the confidence of any nobleman who employed him. Therefore he himself must have been.

"Then perhaps you can tell me whether he was entangled with a woman," said Mr. Flexen.

"Entangled? In what way?" said Mr. Manley in a tone of surprise.

"In the usual way, I suppose. Was he engaged in a love-affair with any woman, or had he been?"

"He certainly did not tell me anything about it if he was," said Mr. Manley. "But that is the kind of thing he might very well *not* confide to his secretary."

"You don't happen to know if he was making any payments to a woman—an allowance, for example?" said Mr. Flexen.

Mr. Manley was well on his guard by now. These questions must surely refer to Helena.

"He never told me anything about it," he said with perfect readiness. "Not, of course, that I would tell you if he had," he added, in his most amiable voice. "I've told you that I thought that he made enough trouble while he was alive. I won't help him to make trouble now that he's dead."

Mr. Flexen thought that the asseveration was unnecessary, since Mr. Manley had not the knowledge which would make the trouble. He returned to the lawyer and told him that Mr. Manley had no information to give.

"It seems a very important point in the affair," said the lawyer.

"It is," said Mr. Flexen, frowning. "I wonder if there was an intrigue with a country girl or woman, someone in the neighbourhood?"

"There might have been. Lord Loudwater rode a great deal. He was hours in the saddle every day. He had time and opportunity for that kind of thing."

"On the other hand, there's no need for it to have been anyone in the neighbourhood at all. To say nothing of the train, it's a short enough motor drive from London; and it was a moonlight night," said Mr. Flexen.

"Then you may be able to find traces of the car. The woman must have left it somewhere while she had the interview with Lord Loudwater," said Mr. Carrington.

"I'll try," said Mr. Flexen, not very hopefully, "But there are so few people about at night nowadays. Five out of the eight gamekeepers are still abroad. In ordinary times there would have been four at least of them about the roads and woods. On that night there was only one."

"There's the further difficulty that Lord Loudwater had so few friends. That will make it harder to find out anything about an affair of this kind–if he had one," said Mr. Carrington.

"It will, indeed," said Mr. Flexen, and paused, frowning. Then he added gravely: "I'm sure that there was such an affair, and I've got to find the woman."

11

Mr. Manley did not lunch with Mr. Flexen and the lawyer. In cultivating Mr. Flexen he had been forced to see less than usual of Helena, and, interesting a companion as Mr. Flexen was, Mr. Manley very much preferred her society. He found her less nervous than she had been the day before, but she still wore a sufficiently anxious air, and was still restless. She seemed more pleased to see him than usual, and the warmth of her welcome gave him a sudden sense that she was even fonder of him than he had thought, or hoped. It stirred him to an admirable response.

At lunch she questioned him with uncommon particularity about the proceedings of Mr. Flexen, the discoveries he had made, the lines on which he was making his investigation. Her interest seemed natural enough, and he told her all that he knew, which was little. She seemed much disappointed by his lack of information. He was careful not to tell her that Mr. Flexen had inquired of him whether he knew of any entanglement between Lord Loudwater and a woman. Thanks to his imagination he was a young man of uncommon discretion, and it was plain that she was suffering anxiety enough.

At the end of her fruitless questioning she sighed and said: "Of course, the whole affair is of no great interest to you really."

"It isn't of very great interest to me," said Mr. Manley. "You see, the victim of the crime, if it was a crime, was such an uninteresting creature. Nature, as I've told you before, intended him for a bull, changed her mind when it was too late to make a satisfactory alteration, and botched it. You must admit that the bull man is a very dull kind of creature, unless he can make things lively for you by prodding you with his horns. When he is dead, he is certainly done with."

"I wish he was done with," she said, with a sigh.

"Well, as far as you are concerned, he is done with, surely," he said, in some surprise.

"Of course, of course," she said quickly. "But still, he seems likely to give a great deal of trouble to somebody; and if there is a trial, how am I to know that my name won't be brought up?"

"I don't think there's a chance of it," he said. "How should it be brought up?"

"One never knows," she said, with a note of nervous dread in her voice.

"Well, as far as I'm concerned, he'll get no help in making a posthumous nuisance of himself from me; and I'm inclined to think that, as things are going, he'll need my help to do that," he said in a tone of quiet satisfaction.

"A posthumous nuisance—you do have phrases! And how you do dislike him!" she said.

"The moderately civilized man, with a gentle disposition like mine, always does hate the bull man. Also, he despises him," said Mr. Manley calmly.

She was silent a while, thinking; then she said: "What did you mean by saying: 'If it was a crime.' What else could it have been?"

"A suicide. The evidence was that the wound might have been self-inflicted," said Mr. Manley.

"Absurd! Lord Loudwater was the last man in the world to commit suicide!" she cried.

"That's purely a matter of individual opinion. I am of the opinion that a man of his uncontrollable temper was quite likely to commit suicide," he said firmly. "As for its being absurd, if there is any attempt to prove anyone guilty of murdering him on purely circumstantial evidence, that person won't find anything absurd in the theory at all. In fact, he'll work it for all it's worth. I think myself that, with Dr. Thornhill's evidence in mind, the police, or the Public Prosecutor, or the Treasury, or whoever it is that decides those things, will never attempt in this case to bring anyone to trial for the murder on merely circumstantial evidence."

"Do you think not?" she said in a tone of relief.

"I'm sure of it," said Mr. Manley. "But why do we waste our time talking about the tiresome fellow when there are things a thousand times more interesting to talk about? Your eyes, now—"

Mr. Flexen instructed Inspector Perkins and his men to make inquiries about the rides of Lord Loudwater and to try to learn whether anyone had seen a strange car, or, indeed, a car of any kind, in the neighbourhood of the Castle about eleven o'clock on the night of the murder. Also, he could see his way to using the newspaper men to help him to discover whether there had been any entanglement known to the club gossips or the people of the neighbourhood between Lord Loudwater and a lady in London. It was not unlikely that he had talked of it to someone, for if they quarrelled so furiously he must need sympathy; and if he had not talked, the lady probably had, though it might very well be that she was not in the circle in which the Loudwaters moved in London. He had some doubt, however, that she was a London woman at all. She had shown too intimate a knowledge of Lord Loudwater's habits at Loudwater and of the Castle itself, for it was clear from William Roper's story that she had gone straight to the library window and through it, in the evident expectation of finding Lord Loudwater asleep as usual in his smoking-room. It was this doubt which prevented him from appealing to Scotland Yard for help in clearing up this particular point. He wished to make sure first that the woman did not belong to the neighbourhood. On the other hand, she might always be someone who had been a guest at the Castle.

He was about to go in search of Lady Loudwater to question her about their friends and acquaintances who might have this knowledge of the Castle and the habits of her husband, when the sleuth from the *Wire* and the sleuth from the *Planet* arrived together, in all amity and the same vexation at being prevented by this errand from spending the afternoon at the same bridge table. The sleuth of the *Wire* was a very solemn-looking young man, with a round, simple face. The sleuth of the *Planet* was a tall, dark man, with an impatient and slightly worried air, who looked uncommonly like an irritable actor-manager.

Both of them greeted Mr. Flexen with affectionate warmth, and Douglas, the tall sleuth of the *Planet*, at once deplored, with considerable bitterness, the fact that he had been robbed of his afternoon's bridge. Gregg, the sleuth of the *Wire*, preserved a gently-blinking, sympathetic silence.

Mr. Flexen at once sent for whisky, soda and cigars, and over them took his two friends into his confidence. He told them that it was very doubtful whether it was a case of murder or suicide; that the jury's verdict was not in accordance with the directions of the Coroner, but just a piece of natural, pig-headed stupidity. This produced another bitter outcry from Douglas about the loss of his afternoon. Mr. Flexen did not soothe him at all by pointing out that he was in a beautiful country on a beautiful day. Then he told them about the coming of the mysterious woman and her violent quarrel with the Lord Loudwater just about the probable time of his death. Douglas at once lost his irritated air and displayed a lively interest in the matter; Gregg listened and blinked. Mr. Flexen told them also of Hutchings, his threats, and his visit to the Castle. That was as far as his confidences went. But they were enough. He had given them the very things they wanted, and they both assured him that they would at once inform him of any discoveries they might make themselves. They left him feeling sure that he might safely leave the servants and the villagers to them and the policemen. If anyone in the neighbourhood knew anything about the mysterious woman, they would probably ferret it out. What was far more important was that tomorrow's *Wire* and *Planet* would contain such an advertisement of her that anyone in London or the country who knew of her relations with the dead man would learn at once the value of that knowledge.

When they had gone he sent for Mrs. Carruthers, and learned, to his annoyance, that none of the upper servants except Elizabeth Twitcher had been in service at the Castle for more than four months. She could only say that during the six weeks that she had been housekeeper there had been very few visitors; and they had been merely callers, except when Colonel Grey had been coming to the Castle and there had been small tennis parties. She had heard nothing from the servants about his lordship's being on particularly friendly terms with any lady in the neighbourhood. Hutchings would be the most likely person to know a thing like that. He had been in service at the Castle all his life. Of course, her ladyship, too, she might know.

Mr. Flexen made up his mind to seek out Hutchings at once and question him on the matter; but Mrs. Carruthers had only just left him when he saw Olivia come into the rose-garden with Colonel Grey. He watched them idly and perceived that, for the time being at any rate, Olivia had lost her strained and anxious air. She was plainly enough absorbed, wholly absorbed, in Grey. She had eyes only for him, and Mr. Flexen suspected that her ears were at the moment deaf to everything but the sound of his voice. They did look a well-matched pair.

It occurred to him that he might as well again question Olivia about her husband's possible intrigue with another woman and be done with it. There could be no harm in Colonel Grey's hearing the questions. As for interrupting their pleasant converse, he thought that

they would soon recover from the interruption.
Accordingly he went out to the rose-garden.

Absorbed in one another, they did not see him till he
was right on them, and then he saw a curious happening.
At the sight of him a sudden, simultaneous apprehension
filled both their faces, and they drew closer together. But
he had an odd fancy that they did not draw together for
mutual protection, but mutually to protect. Then, almost
on the instant, they were gazing at him with politely
inquiring eyes, Lady Loudwater smiling. He felt that they
were intensely on their guard. It was uncommonly
puzzling.

He changed his mind about questioning Lady
Loudwater in the presence of Grey, and asked if she could
spare him a minute or two to answer a few questions.

"Oh, yes. I'm sure Colonel Grey will excuse me," she
said readily.

"But why shouldn't you question Lady Loudwater
before me?" said Colonel Grey coolly; but he slapped his
thigh nervously with the pair of gloves he was carrying.
"It's always as well for a woman to have a man at hand in
an awkward affair like this, which may lead to a good
deal of unpleasantness if anything goes wrong. I'm a
friend of Lady Loudwater, and I don't suppose you fear
that anything you discuss before me will go any further,
Mr. Flexen."

He was cool enough, but Mr. Flexen did not miss the
note of anxiety in his voice.

"I don't mind at all if Lady Loudwater would like it,"
he said readily. "But it's rather a delicate matter."

"Oh, I should like Colonel Grey to hear everything,"
said Olivia quickly.

"It's about the matter of an entanglement between
Lord Loudwater and some lady. Are you quite sure there
was nothing of the kind before his marriage, if not after
it?" said Mr. Flexen.

"I don't know for certain," said Olivia readily. "But
two or three times Lord Loudwater did talk about other

women in a boasting sort of way. Only it was when he was trying to annoy me; so I didn't pay much attention to it."

"And you never tried to find out whether it was the truth or not?" said Mr. Flexen.

"No, never. You see, I didn't particularly care," said Olivia, with unexpected frankness. "If I'd cared, I expect it would have been very different."

"And did Lord Loudwater never mention the name of any lady when he was boasting?" said Mr. Flexen.

"No. Never. It was just general boasting. And he certainly gave me to understand that it was two or three, not one," said Olivia.

"Have you any suspicion that he had any particular lady in mind—any of your common friends, for example—someone who has stayed at the Castle?" said Mr. Flexen.

"None at all. I haven't the slightest idea who it could have been. It must have been someone I don't know, or I should have been nearly sure to notice something," said Olivia.

"Can you tell me anyone who might know?"

Olivia shook her head, and said: "No. I don't know any friend of my husband well enough to say. He never told me who his chief friends were. It never occurred to me that he had an intimate friend. I always thought he hadn't, in fact."

"I tell you what: you might inquire of Outhwaite, you know the man I mean, the man who used always to be getting fined for furious driving. He was a friend of Loudwater, the only friend I ever heard him mention, indeed. If he ever confided in anyone, that would be the most likely man," said Colonel Grey.

"Thank you. That's an idea. I'll certainly try him," said Mr. Flexen, and he turned as if to go.

But Olivia stopped him, saying: "Do you think, then, that a woman did it, Mr. Flexen?"

"Well, there is a certain amount of evidence which lends some colour to that theory, but I don't want anyone to know that," said Mr. Flexen.

And then he could have sworn that he heard Olivia breathe a faint sigh of relief.

But Colonel Grey broke in in a tone of some acerbity and more anxiety:

"It's nonsense to talk of anyone having done it in face of the medical evidence—anyone, that is, but Loudwater himself. He committed suicide."

"You think him a likely man to have committed suicide, do you?" said Mr. Flexen.

"Yes. A man of his utterly uncontrollable temper is the very man to commit suicide," said Colonel Grey firmly.

"It is, of course, always possible that he committed suicide," said Mr. Flexen in a non-committal tone.

"It's most probable," said Colonel Grey curtly.

"What do you think, Lady Loudwater?" said Flexen.

"Why, I haven't thought much about it. I always—I—but now I do think about it, I—I—think it's not unlikely," said Olivia, in a tone of no great conviction. "And he was so frightfully upset, too, that night—not that he had any reason to be; but he was."

"Ah, well; my duty is to investigate the matter till there isn't a shadow of doubt left," said Mr. Flexen in a pleasant voice. "I daresay that I shall get to the bottom of it."

With that he left them and went back into the Castle.

At the sight of his back Olivia breathed so deep a sigh of relief that Grey winced at it.

"If only it could be proved that Egbert did commit suicide!" she said wistfully.

"I don't see any chance of it," said Colonel Grey gloomily. Then he added in a tone of but faint hope: "Unless he wrote to one of his friends that he intended to commit suicide."

Olivia shook her head and said: "Egbert wouldn't do that. He hated letter-writing."

"Besides, if he had, we should have heard of it by now," said Grey.

"The friend might be away," said Olivia. "I know that Mr. Outhwaite was in France."

"That's hoping too much," said Grey.

They strolled on in silence, his eyes on her thoughtful face, which under Mr. Flexen's questioning had again grown anxious. Then he said: "This sun is awfully hot. Let's stroll through the wood to the pavilion. It will be delightful there."

"Very well," said Olivia, smiling at him.

Mr. Flexen went back to his room, rang for Holloway, and bade him find Mr. Manley, if he were in, and ask him to come to him. Holloway went, and presently returned to say that Mr. Manley had gone out to lunch, but left word that he would be back to dinner.

Mr. Flexen, therefore, gave his mind to the consideration of his talk with Colonel Grey and Olivia, and the longer he considered it, the more their attitude intrigued and puzzled him. They certainly knew something about the murder, something of the first importance. What could it be?

Again he asked himself could either, or both of them, have actually had a hand in it? It seemed improbable; but he was used to the improbable happening. He could not believe that either of them would have dreamt of committing murder to gain a personal end—to save themselves, for example, from the injuries with which Lord Loudwater had threatened them. But would they commit murder to save someone else, one to save the other, for example, from such an injury? Murder was, indeed, a violent measure; but Mr. Flexen was inclined to think that either of them might take it. Mr. Manley's confident declaration that they were both creatures of strong emotions had impressed him. He felt that Colonel

Grey, under the impulse to save Lady Loudwater, would stick at very little; and he was used to violence and to hold human life cheap. On the other hand, Lady Loudwater would go a long way—a very long way—if anyone she loved were threatened. The fact that she had good Italian blood in her veins was very present in his mind.

Again, it would be a matter of sudden impulse, not of grave deliberation. The irritating sound of Lord Loudwater's snores and the sight of the gleaming knife-blade on the library table coming together after their painful and moving discussion of their dangers might awake the impulse to be rid of him, at any cost, in full strength. He was not disposed to underrate the suggestion of that naked knife-blade on them when they were strung to such a height of emotion. Again, he asked himself, had either of them murdered Lord Loudwater to save the other?

At any rate, they knew who had committed the murder. Of that he was sure.

Could they be shielding a third person? If so, who was that third person?

12

Mr. Flexen sat pondering this question of a third person for a good twenty minutes.

It could not be Hutchings. There would be no reason to shield Hutchings unless they had instigated or employed him to commit the murder, and that was out of the question. He was not sure, indeed, that Hutchings was not the murderer; the snores and the knife were as likely to have excited the murderous impulse in him as in them. He was quite sure that if Dr. Thornhill had been able to swear that the wound was not self-inflicted, he could have secured the conviction of Hutchings. But it was incredible that Lady Loudwater or Colonel Grey had employed him to commit the murder. No; if they were shielding a third person, it must be the mysterious, unknown woman who had come with such swift secrecy and so wholly disappeared.

It grew clearer and clearer that there most probably lay that solution of the problem. If that woman herself had not murdered Lord Loudwater, as seemed most likely, she might very well give him the clue for which he was groping. He must find her, and, of course, sooner or later he would find her. But the sooner he found her, the sooner would the problem be solved and his work done. Till he found her he would not find its solution.

It still seemed to him probable that somewhere among Lord Loudwater's papers there was information which would lead to her discovery, and he went into the library to confer again with Mr. Carrington on the matter. He found him discussing the arrangements for tomorrow's funeral with Mrs. Carruthers and Wilkins.

When they had gone he said: "Did you come across any information about that mysterious woman in the rest of the papers?"

"Not a word," said Mr. Carrington.

"I've been thinking that you might come across traces of her in his pass-books–payments or an allowance."

"I thought of that. But there's only one passbook, the one in use. Lord Loudwater doesn't seem to have kept them after they were filled. And Manley knows all about this one; he wrote out every cheque in it for Loudwater, and he is quite sure that there were no cheques of any size for a woman among them."

"That's disappointing," said Mr. Flexen. "What about the cheques to 'Self'? Are there any large ones among them?"

"No. They're all on the small side–distinctly on the small side–cheques for ten pounds–and very few of them."

"It is queer that it should be so difficult to find any information about a woman who played such an important part in his life," said Mr. Flexen gloomily.

"It's not so very uncommon," said the lawyer.

"Well, let's hope that the advertisement she'll get from my newspaper friends will bring her to light," said Mr. Flexen.

"It would be a pleasant surprise to me to find them serving some useful purpose," said Mr. Carrington grimly.

Mr. Flexen laughed and said: "You're prejudiced. It's about time to dress for dinner."

Mr. Carrington rose with alacrity and said anxiously, "I hope to goodness Loudwater didn't quarrel with his chef!"

"I've no reason to think so. The food's excellent," said Mr. Flexen.

Mr. Manley joined them at dinner, wearing his best air of a discreet and indulgent man of the world, and confident of making himself valued. He was in very good spirits, for he had persuaded Helena to marry him that day month, and was rejoicing in his success. He did not tell Mr. Flexen, or Mr. Carrington, of his good fortune. He felt that it would hardly interest them, since neither of them knew Helena or was intimate with himself. But, inspired by this success, he took the lead in the conversation, and showed himself inclined to be somewhat patronizing to two men outside the sphere of imaginative literature.

It was Mr. Flexen who broached the subject of the murder.

After they had talked of the usual topics for a while, he said: "By the way, Manley, did you hear Lord Loudwater snore after Hutchings went into the library, or before?"

"So you know that I saw Hutchings in the hall that night?" said Mr. Manley. "It's wonderful how you find things out. I didn't tell you, and I should have thought that I was the only person awake in the front part of the Castle. I suppose that someone saw him getting his cigarettes from the butler's pantry."

"So that was the reason he gave you for being in the Castle," said Mr. Flexen. "Well, was it after or before you spoke to him that you heard Lord Loudwater snore?"

Mr. Manley hesitated, thinking; then he said: "I can't remember at the moment. You see, I was downstairs some little time. I found an evening paper in the dining-room and looked through it there. I might have heard him from there."

"You can't remember?" said Mr. Flexen in a tone of disappointment.

"Not at the moment," said Mr. Manley. "Is it important?"

"Yes; very important. It would probably help me to fix the time of Lord Loudwater's death."

"I see. A lot may turn on that," said Mr. Manley thoughtfully.

"Yes. You can see how immensely it helps to have a fact like that fixed," said Mr. Flexen.

"Yes: of course," said Mr. Manley. "Well, I must try to remember. I daresay I shall, if I keep the fact in my mind gently, and do not try to wrench the recollection out of it. You know how hard it is to remember a thing, if it hasn't caught your attention fairly when it happened."

"Yes," said Mr. Flexen. "But I hope to goodness you'll remember it quickly. It may be of the greatest use to me."

"Ah, yes; I must," said Mr. Manley, giving him a queer look.

"I was forgetting," said Mr. Flexen, understanding the thought behind the queer look. "You'd hardly believe it, Mr. Carrington, but Mr. Manley told me at the very beginning of this business that he was not going to help in any way to discover the murderer of Lord Loudwater, because he considered that murderer a benefactor of society."

"But I never heard of such a thing!" cried the lawyer in a tone of astonished disapproval. "Such a course might be possible in the case of some minor crime, or in a person intimately connected with the criminal in the case of a major crime. But for an outsider to pursue such a course in the case of a murder is unheard of—absolutely unheard of."

"I daresay it isn't common," said Mr. Manley in a tone of modest satisfaction. "But I am modern; I claim the right of private judgment in all matters of morality."

"Oh, that won't do—that won't do at all!" cried the shocked lawyer. "There would be hopeless confusion—in fact, if everybody did that, the law might easily become a dead letter—absolutely a dead letter."

"But there's no fear of everybody doing anything of the kind. The ruck of men have no private judgment to claim the right of. They take whatever's given them in the way of morals by their pastors and masters. Only exceptional people have ideas of their own to carry out;

and there are not enough exceptional people to make much difference," said Mr. Manley calmly.

"But, all the same, such principles are subversive of society—absolutely subversive of society," said Mr. Carrington warmly, and his square, massive face was growing redder.

"I daresay," said Mr. Manley amiably. "But if anyone chooses to have them, and act on them, what are you going to do about it? For example, if I happened to know who had murdered Lord Loudwater and did not choose to tell, how could you make me?"

"If there were many people with such principles about, society would soon find out a way of protecting itself," said the lawyer, in the accents of one whose tenderest sensibilities are being outraged.

"It would have to have recourse to torture then," said Mr. Manley cheerfully.

"But let me remind you that it is a crime to be an accessory before, or after, the fact to murder," said the lawyer in a tone of some triumph.

"Oh, I'm not going as far as that," said Mr. Manley. "A man might very well approve of a murder without being willing to further it."

Mr. Flexen laughed and said: "I understand Mr. Manley's point of view. Sometimes I have felt inclined to be judge as well as investigator—especially in the East."

"And you followed your inclination," said Mr. Manley with amiable certainty.

"Perhaps—perhaps not," said Mr. Flexen, smiling at him.

"The war has upset everything. I never heard such ideas before the war," grumbled the lawyer.

There was a silence as Holloway brought in the coffee and cigars.

When he had gone, Mr. Flexen said in an almost fretful tone: "It's an extraordinary thing that Lord Loudwater kept so few papers."

"I don't know," said Mr. Manley carelessly. "During the six months I've been here we were never stuck for want of a paper. He seemed to me to have kept all that were necessary."

"It's the destroying of his pass-books that seems so odd to me," said the lawyer. "A man must often want to know how he spent his money in a given year."

"I'm sure I never want to," said Mr. Manley. "And certainly pass-books are unattractive-looking objects to have about."

"All the same, they might have proved very useful in this case," said Mr. Flexen. "Of course, they wouldn't tell us anything we shall not find out eventually. But they might have saved us a lot of time and trouble. They might put us on to the track of another firm of lawyers who did certain business for Lord Loudwater."

"Well, no one but Mr. Carrington's firm did any business for him during the last six months," said Mr. Manley, rising. "I feel inclined to take advantage of the moonlight and go for a stroll. So I will leave you to go on working on the murder. Good-bye for the present."

He sauntered out of the room, and when the door closed behind him, the lawyer said earnestly: "I do hate a crank."

The words came from his heart.

"Oh, I don't think he's a crank," said Mr. Flexen in an indulgent tone. "He's too intelligent; that's all."

"There's nothing so dangerous as too much intelligence. It's always a nuisance to other people," said the lawyer. "Do you think he really knows anything?"

"He knows something—nothing of real importance, I think," said Mr. Flexen. "But, as I expect you've noticed, he likes to feel himself of importance. And whatever knowledge he has helps him to feel important. It's a harmless hobby. By the way, is there anything in the way of insanity in Lady Loudwater's family?"

"No, I never heard of any, and I should have been almost certain to hear if there were any," said the lawyer in some surprise.

"That's all right," said Mr. Flexen.

"By the way, how did you get on with the newspaper men?" said the lawyer.

"I put them in the way of making themselves very useful to me, and, at the same time, I gave them exactly the kind of thing they wanted. I think, too, that when they've run the story I gave them for all it's worth, they'll very likely drop the case—unless, that is, we've really got it cleared up. I was careful to point out to them that the verdict of the coroner's jury was a piece of pig-headed idiocy, and they'll see the unlikelihood of securing a conviction for murder with the medical evidence as it is, unless we have an absolutely clear case."

"But, all the same, there's going to be a tremendous fuss in the papers," said Mr. Carrington, in the tone of dissatisfaction of the lawyer who is always doing his best to keep tremendous fusses out of the papers.

"Oh, yes. That was necessary. It's out of that fuss that I hope to get the evidence which will settle once and for all, in my mind at any rate, the question whether Lord Loudwater was murdered or not."

"But surely you haven't any doubt about that?" said the lawyer sharply.

"Just a trifle, and I may as well get rid of it," said Mr. Flexen.

Mr. Manley took his hat and stick and went leisurely out of the front door of the Castle. He paused on the steps for half a minute to admire the moonlit night and murmur a few lines from Keats. Then he strolled down the drive whistling the tune of an American coon song. But presently the whistle died on his lips as he considered Mr. Flexen's keen desire to discover the other firm of lawyers who had done business for Lord Loudwater. He could not but think, when he put this keenness of Mr. Flexen beside Helena's strange anxiety, that she had done something of which she had not told him, something that might have drawn suspicion on her. He did not see what she could have done; but there it was. He had a feeling, an intuition that it was she whom Mr. Flexen was seeking, and he prided himself on his intuition. Well, the longer they were finding Shepherd, the lawyer who had handled the business of her allowance, the better he would be pleased. He had certainly done his best to block their way. At the same time, they might at any moment learn who he was. It was fortunate, therefore, that Shepherd had a job in Mesopotamia, and that his business was closed down for the present. If they did learn who he was, they would still be a long while before they obtained any information about Helena from him. Mr. Manley's keen desire was that the first excitement about the murder should have died down before they did get it. He was a firm believer in the soothing effect of time. The discovery of Helena's allowance, if it were made now, might cause her considerable annoyance, if not actual trouble. Coming in six weeks' time, or even a month's time, it would be far less likely to make that trouble.

He wondered what it could be that she had done to bring herself under suspicion. Remembering what she had said of her determination to discuss the halving of her allowance with the dead man, and her remark that she had such a knowledge of his habits that she could make sure of having an interview with him to discuss it, it seemed not unlikely that she had gone to see him on the very night of his murder, and that someone had seen her. If it were so, he hoped that she would tell him, so that they might together devise some way of preventing harm coming from the accident that the interview had occurred at such an unfortunate hour. He felt sure that he would be able to devise such a way. He never blinked the fact of his extreme ingenuity.

He found her strolling in her garden with the anxious frown which had awakened his uneasiness, still on her brow. Her face grew brighter at the sight of him, and presently he had smoothed the frown quite away. Again he realized that the murder of Lord Loudwater had had a softening effect on her. Before it they had been much more on equality; now she rather clung to him. He found it pleasing, much more the natural attitude of a woman towards a man of his imagination and knowledge of life. He was properly gracious and protective with her.

The next morning the *Daily Wire* opened his eyes and confirmed his apprehensions. The murder of a nobleman is an uncommon occurrence, and the editor of that paper showed every intention of making the most of it. The visit of the unknown woman to Lord Loudwater and their quarrel, treated with the nervous picturesqueness of which Mr. Gregg was so famous a master, formed the main and interesting part of the article. When he came to the end of it, Mr. Manley whistled ruefully. He had no difficulty whatever in picturing to himself the indignant and violent wrath of Helena, and he could not conceive for a moment that Lord Loudwater had been able to withstand it. Of course, he would be violent, too, but with a much less impressive violence.

Lord Loudwater had been lavish in the matter of newspapers; he was a rich man, and they had been his only reading. Mr. Manley read the report of the inquest in all the chief London dailies, and found in the *Daily Planet* another nervously picturesque article on the visit of the mysterious woman from the nervously picturesque pen of Mr. Douglas.

Here was certainly a pretty kettle of fish. He could not doubt that the woman was Helena. It explained Flexen's questioning him whether he had any knowledge of an entanglement between Lord Loudwater and a woman, and Flexen's keen desire to find some other firm of lawyers who might have been called in to deal with such an entanglement. But he could not for a moment bring himself to believe that there could have ever been any need for Helena to have recourse to the knife. He could not see Lord Loudwater resisting her when she became really angry; he must have given way. None the less, he did not underestimate the awkwardness, the danger even, of her having paid that visit and had that quarrel at such an unfortunate hour.

He had matter enough for earnest thought during the funeral. It was a large funeral, though there were not many funeral guests. Five ladies, an aunt and four cousins, of Lord Loudwater's own generation, came down from London. The younger generation was either on its way back from the war, or too busy with its work to find the time to attend the funeral of a distant relation, whom, if they had chanced to meet him, they neither liked nor respected. But there was a show of carriages from all the big houses within a radius of nine miles, which more than made up for the fewness of the guests. Also, there was a crowd of middle- and lower-class spectators who considered the funeral of a murdered nobleman a spectacle indeed worth attending. It was composed of women, children, old men, and a few wounded private soldiers.

Olivia attended the funeral, wearing a composed but rather pathetic air, owing to the fact that her brow was most of the time knitted in a pondering, troubled frown. Lady Croxley, Lord Loudwater's aged aunt, rode with her in the first coach. She was a loquacious soul, and whiled away the journey to and from the church, which is over a mile from the Castle, with a panegyric on her dead nephew, and an astonished dissertation on the strange fact that Olivia had not had a woman with her during this sad time. She ascribed her abstinence from this stimulant to her desire to be alone with her grief. Olivia encouraged her harmless babble by a vague murmur at the right points, and continued to look pathetic. It was all her aunt by marriage needed, and it left Olivia free to think her own thoughts. She gave but few of them to her dead husband; the living claimed her attention.

Mr. Manley wore an air of gloom far deeper than his sense of the fitness of things would in the ordinary course of events have demanded. It was the result of the nervously picturesque English which had flowed with such ease from the forceful pens of Mr. Douglas and Mr. Gregg. Mr. Carrington, who rode with him, and from attending the funerals of many clients had acquired as good a funeral air as any man in his profession, found his gloom exaggerated. He was all the more scandalized, therefore, when, as they were nearing the Castle, Mr. Manley suddenly cried, "By Jove!" and rubbed his hands together with a face uncommonly radiant.

He had had the cheering thought that he had the Loudwater case, if ever it should come to a trial, wholly in his hands. He had but to remember having heard Lord Loudwater snore at, say, a few minutes to twelve, to break it down. He did not conceive that he would encounter any difficulty in remembering that if it should be necessary.

The solemnity of the funeral and Mr. Carrington's conversation in the coach–he had talked about the weather–had not weakened his resolve that, if he could help it, no one should swing for the murder.

This realization of his position of vantage made him eager to go to Helena to set her mind at rest, should she, as he thought most likely, be greatly troubled by the fact that her untimely visit to the murdered man was known. But he had to lunch at the Castle with the funeral guests. They were interested beyond measure in the murder and full of questions. He talked to them with a darkly mysterious air, and made a deep impression of discreet sagacity on their simple minds. He observed that Olivia appeared to have been afflicted more deeply by the funeral than he had expected. She looked harassed and seemed to find the lunch rather a strain. He observed also that she did not, as did her guests, who were so slightly acquainted with him, pay any tribute to the character of her dead husband.

Mr. Flexen was not lunching with them. He had spent an expectant morning waiting for the local effects of the story in the *Wire* and *Planet*, and in having that story spread far and wide by Inspector Perkins and his two men among the villagers, who only saw a paper in the public-houses of the neighbourhood on a Sunday. He hoped, if it had been a local affair, to have information about it in the course of the day. Up to lunchtime the newspaper advertisement of the mysterious woman had proved as fruitless as the earlier private inquiries. But he remained hopeful.

It was past three before Mr. Manley escaped from the funeral guests and betook himself at a brisk pace to Helena's house. As he went he made up his mind that the quality most fitting the occasion was discretion. He had better not let it appear that he was sure that she was the mysterious woman of the *Daily Wire*. He must make his announcement that, in the event of anyone being brought to trial for the murder of Lord Loudwater, his evidence could break down any case for the prosecution, and that he would see that it did break it down, appear as casual as possible. But, at the same time, he must make it quite clear to her that he could secure her safety. He felt that though she might think his firm resolve that no one should swing for the murder quixotic, she would perceive that it was only in keeping with his generous nature.

He had expected to find her much more disturbed by the nervously picturesque articles of Mr. Gregg and Mr. Douglas than she appeared. Indeed, she seemed to him much less under a strain, much less nervous than she had been the night before. None the less, he was careful to reassure her wholly by the announcement of his discovery of the important nature of the evidence he could give, before he said anything about those articles. When he did tell her that he could break down any case for the prosecution, she did not at once confess that she was the woman of whose visit to Lord Loudwater those stories told; they did not even discuss the question, which had seemed so important to the *Daily Wire,* who that woman was. They contented themselves with discussing the question who could have seen her. He admired her spirit in not telling him, her readiness to forgo his comfort and support before the absolute need for them was upon her. Her force of character was what he most admired in her, and this was a striking example of it. His own character, he knew, was rather subtile and delicate than strong. He was more than ever alive to the advantage of having her to lean upon in the difficult career that lay before him.

Mr. Flexen was disappointed that the advertisement of the mysterious woman in the *Wire* and the *Planet* brought no information about her during the morning. After lunch Mr. Carrington returned to London. At half-past three Mr. Flexen telegraphed to Scotland Yard to ask if anyone had given them information about the woman he was seeking. No one had. Then he realized that he was unreasonably impatient. Whoever had the information would probably think the matter over, and perhaps confer with friends before coming forward. In the meantime, he would make inquiries of James Hutchings.

He drove to the gamekeeper's cottage to find James Hutchings sitting on a chair outside it and reading the *Planet.* He perceived that he looked puzzled. Also, he perceived that he still wore a strained, hunted air, more strained and hunted by far than at their last talk.

He walked briskly up to him and said: "Good afternoon. I see that you're reading the story of Lord Loudwater's murder in the *Planet.* It occurred to me that you might very likely be able to tell me who the lady who visited Lord Loudwater on the night of his murder was. At any rate, you can probably make a guess at who she was."

Hutchings shook his head and said gloomily: "No, sir, I can't. I don't know who it was and I can't guess. I wish I could. I'd tell you like a shot."

"That's odd," said Mr. Flexen, again disappointed. "I should have thought it impossible for your master to have been on intimate terms with a lady without your coming to hear of it. You've always been his butler."

"Yes, sir. But this is the kind of thing as a valet gets to know about more than a butler—letters left about, or in pockets, you know, sir. But his lordship never could keep a valet long enough for him to learn anything. He was worse with valets than with anyone."

"I see," said Mr. Flexen in a vexed tone. "But still, I should have thought you'd have heard something from someone, even if the matter had not come under your own eyes. Gossip moves pretty widely about the countryside."

"Oh, this didn't happen in the country, sir—not in this part of the country, anyhow. It must have been a London woman," said Hutchings with conviction. "If she'd lived about here, I must have heard about it."

"It was a lady, you must know. The papers do not bring that fact out. My informant is quite sure that it was a lady," said Mr. Flexen.

"That's no 'elp, sir," said Hutchings despondently. "She must have come down by train and gone away by train."

"She would have probably been noticed at the station. But she wasn't. Besides, she could not have walked back to the station in time to catch the last train. I'm sure of it."

"Then she must have come in a car, sir."

"That is always possible," said Mr. Flexen.

There was a pause.

Then Hutchings burst out: "You may depend on it that she did it, sir. There isn't a shadow of a doubt. You get her and you'll get the murderess."

He spoke with the feverish, unbalanced vehemence of a man whose nerves are on edge.

"You think so, do you?" said Mr. Flexen.

"I'm sure of it–dead certain," cried Hutchings.

"It's a long way from visiting a gentleman late at night and quarrelling with him to murdering him," said Mr. Flexen.

"And she went it. You mark my words, sir. She went it. I don't say that she came to do it. But she saw that knife lying handy on the library table and she did it," said Hutchings with the same vehemence.

"Anyone who passed through the library would see that knife," said Mr. Flexen carelessly, but his eyes were very keen on Hutchings' face.

Hutchings was pale, and he went paler. He tried to stammer something, but his voice died in his throat.

"Well, I'm sorry you can't give me any information about this lady. Good afternoon," said Mr. Flexen, and he turned on his heel and went back to the car.

He was impressed by Hutchings' air and manner. Of course, believing himself to be suspected, the man was under a strain. But would the strain on him be so heavy as it plainly was, if he knew himself to be innocent? And then his eagerness to fasten the crime on the mysterious woman. It had been astonishingly intense, almost hysterical.

When he reached the Castle he found Inspector Perkins awaiting him with a small package which had come by special messenger from Scotland Yard. It contained enlarged photographs of the fingerprints on the handle of the knife. They were all curiously blurred.

The murderer had worn a glove.

13

Mr. Flexen studied the photographs and the report which stated this fact with a lively interest and a growing sense of its great importance. For one thing, it settled the question of suicide for good and all. Lord Loudwater had worn no glove.

Also, it strengthened the case against the mysterious woman. She had come, apparently, from a distance, and probably in a motor-car. If she had driven herself down, she would be wearing gloves. Also, only a woman would be likely to be wearing gloves on a warm summer night. Indeed, coming from a distance by train, or car, she would certainly wear gloves. She would not dream of coming to an interview, with a man with whom she had been intimate and whom she wished to bend to her will, with hands dirtied by a journey.

If that gloved hand had not been the hand of the mysterious woman, then the murder had been premeditated, and the murderer or murderess had put on gloves with the deliberate purpose of leaving no finger-prints.

It *was* the woman. In all probability it was the woman.

Then Mr. Flexen's sub-conscious mind began to jog his intellect. Somewhere in his memory there was a fact he had noted about gloves, and that fact was now important in its bearing on the case. He set about trying to recall it to his mind. He was not long about it. Of a sudden he remembered that he had been a trifle surprised to perceive that Colonel Grey had been carrying gloves when he had found him in the rose-garden with Lady Loudwater.

His surprise had passed quickly enough. He had decided that the life in the trenches had not weakened Colonel Grey's habit, as a fastidious man about town, of taking care of his hands. He remembered, too, that at his first interview with him he had observed that his hands were uncommonly well shaped and well kept.

He did not suppose that Colonel Grey had come to the Castle on the night of the murder wearing gloves with the deliberate intention of killing Lord Loudwater without leaving finger-prints. But suppose that, as he came away from a distressing interview with Lady Loudwater, the knife on the library table had caught his eye and his gloves had been in his pocket?

Mr. Flexen took out his pipe, lit it, and moved to an easy-chair to let his brain work more easily. He tabulated his facts.

Colonel Grey had gone through the library window at about twenty minutes past ten.

Hutchings had gone through the library window at half-past ten.

The mysterious woman had gone through the library window at about ten minutes to eleven.

She came out of the library window at about a quarter-past eleven after a violent quarrel with Lord Loudwater.

Colonel Grey came out of the library window at about twenty-five minutes past eleven, after a distressing interview with Lady Loudwater, apparently in a very bad temper.

James Hutchings had come out of the library window at about half-past eleven, also, if William Roper might be believed, furious.

Lady Loudwater had come through the library window at a quarter to twelve, and gone back through it at five minutes to twelve.

Each of the last three had passed within fifteen feet of Lord Loudwater, dead or alive, both on entering and on coming out of the Castle. The mysterious woman had actually been in the smoking-room with him.

If Lady Loudwater's statement that she heard her husband snoring at five minutes to twelve were to be accepted, neither Colonel Grey, Hutchings, nor the mysterious woman could have committed the murder— unless always one of them had returned later and committed it. That possibility must be borne in mind.

But Mr. Flexen did not accept her statement. If he were to accept it, she herself at once became the most likely person to have committed the crime. It was always possible that she had. She certainly had the best reasons of anyone, as far as he knew, for committing it.

The evidence of Mr. Manley about the time at which he heard Lord Loudwater snore was of the first importance. But how to get it out of him? Mr. Flexen had a strong feeling that not only would Mr. Manley afford no help to bring the murderer of Lord Loudwater to justice, but, that owing to the vein of Quixotry in his nature, he was capable of helping the murderer to escape. That he could do. He had only to declare that he heard Lord Loudwater snore at twelve o'clock to break down the case against anyone of the four persons between whom the crime obviously lay. Mr. Flexen had a shrewd suspicion that Mr. Manley would fail to remember at what time he had last heard Lord Loudwater's snores till the police had set about securing the conviction of one of the possible murderers. Then, when the case of the police against the murderer was revealed, he would come forward and break it down. He had decided that Mr. Manley was a sentimentalist, and he knew well the difficulty of dealing with sentimentalists. Moreover, Mr. Manley was animated by a grudge against the murdered man. Mr. Flexen could quite conceive that he might presently be regarding perjury as a duty; he had had experience of the queer way in which the mind of the sentimentalist works.

It appeared to him that everything depended on his finding the mysterious woman.

That afternoon Elizabeth Twitcher determined to go to see James Hutchings. She had not seen him since their interview on the night of the murder. In the ordinary course she would not have dreamt of going to him after that interview, for it had left them on such a footing that further advances, repentant advances, must come from him. But there were pressing reasons why she should not wait for him to make the advances which he would in ordinary circumstances have made after his sulkiness had abated. All her fellow-servants and all the villagers, who were not members of the Hutchings family, were assured that he had murdered Lord Loudwater. Three of the maids, who were jealous of her greater prettiness, had with ill-dissembled spitefulness congratulated her on having dismissed him before the murder; her mother had also congratulated her on that fact. Elizabeth Twitcher was the last girl in the world to desert a man in misfortune, and, considering James Hutchings' temper, she could only consider the murder a misfortune. Besides, she had been very fond of him; she was very fond of him still, and the fact that he was in great trouble was making him dearer to her.

Moreover, everyone who spoke to her about him told her that he was looking miserable beyond words. Her heart went out to him.

None the less, she did not go to see him without a struggle. She felt that he ought to come to her. However, her pride had been beaten in that struggle by her fondness and her pity—even more by her pity.

When she knocked at the door of his father's cottage James Hutchings himself opened it, and his harassed, hang-dog air settled in her mind for good and all the question of his guilt. She was not daunted; indeed, a sudden anger against Lord Loudwater for having brought about his own murder flamed up in her. Like everyone else who had known him, she could feel no pity for him.

James Hutchings showed no pleasure whatever at the sight of her. Indeed, he scowled at her.

"Come to gloat over me, have you?" he growled bitterly.

"Don't be silly!" she said sharply. "What should I want to do a thing like that for? Is your father in?"

"No; he isn't," said James Hutchings sulkily, but his eyes gazed at her hungrily.

He showed no intention of inviting her to enter. Therefore she pushed past him, walked across the kitchen, sat down in the window-seat, and surveyed him.

He shut the door, turned, and gazed at her, scowling uncertainly.

Then she said gently: "You're looking very poorly, Jim."

"I didn't think you'd be the one to tell of my being in the Castle that night!" he cried bitterly.

"It wasn't me," she said quietly. "It was that little beast, Jane Pittaway. She heard us talking in the drawing-room."

"Oh, that was it, was it?" he said more gently. Then, scowling again, he cried fiercely:

"I'll wring her neck!"

"That's enough of that!" she said sharply. "You've talked a lot too much about wringing people's necks. And a lot of good it's done you."

"Oh, I know you believe I did it, just like everybody else. But I tell you I didn't. I swear I didn't!" he cried loudly, with a vehemence which did not convince her.

"Of course you didn't," she said in a soothing voice. "But what are you going to do if they try to make out that you did? What are you going to tell them?"

He gazed at her with miserable eyes and said in a miserable voice: "God knows what I'm to tell them. It isn't a matter of telling them. It's how to make 'em believe it. These people never believe anything; the police never do."

She gazed at him thoughtfully, with eyes compassionate and full of tenderness. They were a balm to his unhappy spirit.

The hardness slowly vanished from his face. It became merely troubled. He walked quickly across the room, dropped into the seat beside her and put an arm round her.

"You're a damned sight too good for me, Lizzie," he said in a gentler voice than she had ever heard him use before, and he kissed her.

"Poor Jim!" she said. And again: "Poor Jim!"

He trembled, breathing quickly, and held her tight.

After a while he regained control of himself, and sat upright. But he still held her tightly to him with his right arm.

They began to discuss his plight and how he might best defend himself. She was fully as fearful as he. But she did not show it. She must cheer him up, and she kept insisting that the police could not fix the murder on him, that they had nothing to go upon. If they had, they would have already arrested him. Certainly they knew what the servants and the village people were saying. But that was just talk. There wasn't any evidence; there couldn't be any evidence.

Her support and encouragement put a new spirit into him. He had been so alone against the world. His own family, though they had loudly and fiercely protested his innocence to their friends and enemies in the village, had not expressed this faith in him to him.

Indeed, his father had expressed their real belief, when he said to him gloomily: "I always told you that damned temper of yours would get you into trouble, Jim."

Then Elizabeth gave him his tea. After it they talked calmly with an actual approach to cheerfulness till it was time for her to return to the Castle to dress Olivia's hair for dinner. Then she would have it that he should escort her back to the Castle. She declared, truly enough, that he was doing himself no good by moping at the cottage, that people would say that he dare not show himself. He *must* hold his head up.

She insisted also that they should take the long way round, through the village; that people should see them together. She insisted that he should look cheerful, and talk to her all the length of the village street. The looking cheerful helped to lighten his spirit yet more. As they went through the village she kept looking up at him in an affectionate fashion and smiling.

The village was, indeed, taken aback. It had made up its mind that James Hutchings was a pariah to be shunned. It was not only taken aback, it was annoyed. It had no wish that its belief that James Hutchings had murdered Lord Loudwater should be in any way unsettled.

Mrs. Roper, the mother of William Roper and a lifelong enemy of the Hutchings family, summed up the feeling of her neighbours about the behaviour of James Hutchings and Elizabeth.

"Brazen, I call it," she said bitterly.

Before they reached the Castle, Elizabeth had come to feel that during the last three days James Hutchings had changed greatly, and for the better. She had an odd fancy that murdering his master had improved his character; the fear of the police had softened him. Not once did he try to domineer over her. That domineering had been the source of their not infrequent quarrels, for she was not at all of a temper to endure it.

Olivia and Grey had again spent their afternoon in the pavilion in the East wood. Their bearing at times had been oddly like that of Elizabeth and James Hutchings. Now and again they had lapsed from their absorption in one another into a like fearfulness. But, unlike Elizabeth and James Hutchings, neither of them said a word about the murder of Lord Loudwater. But both of them seemed a little less under a strain than they had been. This new factor of a quarrel with an unknown woman seemed to open a loophole. Olivia's colouring had lost some of its warmth; the contours of her face were less rounded. Grey had manifestly taken a step backwards in his convalescence; his face was thinner, even a little haggard; there was a somewhat strained watchfulness in his eyes.

They could not tear themselves away from the pavilion till the last moment, and he walked back with her as far as the shrubbery on the edge of the East lawn, and there they parted after she had promised to meet him there that evening at nine.

As Olivia came into her sitting-room Elizabeth and James Hatchings came to the back door of the Castle. She did not say good-bye at once; of set purpose, she lingered talking to him that the other servants might understand clearly that her attitude to him was definitely fixed.

But at last she held out her hand and said: "I must be getting along to her ladyship, or she'll be waiting for me."

James Hutchings looked round, considered the coast sufficiently clear, caught her to him, kissed her, and said huskily: "You're just a ministering angel, Lizzie, and there's more sense in your little finger than in all my fat head. I'm feeling a different man, and I'll baulk them yet."

"Of course you will, Jim," said Elizabeth, and she opened the door.

"Lord, how I wish I was coming in with you–back in my old place! I should be seeing you most of the time," he said wistfully.

Elizabeth stopped short, flushing, and looked at him with suddenly excited eyes.

At his words a great thought had come into her mind.

"Wait a minute, Jim. Wait till I come back," she said somewhat breathlessly, and, leaving the door open, she hurried down the passage.

She hurried up to her room, took off her hat, and hurried to Olivia. She found her in her sitting-room looking through an evening paper to learn if any new fact about the murder had come to light.

"If you please, your ladyship, James Hutchings has come to ask if your ladyship would like him to come back for the time being till you've got suited with another butler," said Elizabeth in a rather breathless voice.

Olivia looked at Elizabeth's flushed, excited and hopeful face, and smiled.

"Why, have you and James made it up, Elizabeth?" she said.

"Yes, m'lady," said Elizabeth, and the flush deepened in her cheeks.

"Then go and tell him to come back, by all means," said Olivia.

"Thank you, m'lady," said Elizabeth, in accents of profound gratitude, and she ran out of the room.

Olivia smiled and then she sighed. It was pleasant to have given Elizabeth such obviously keen pleasure. She never dreamed that Elizabeth and James Hutchings were under the same strain of fear and anxiety as she herself, and that she had given them great help in their trouble, for Elizabeth saw that the return of James Hutchings to his situation would give the wagging tongues full pause.

James Hutchings was dumbfounded on receiving the message. He stared at Elizabeth with his mouth open.

"Be quick, Jim. Get your clothes and be back in time to wait on her ladyship at dinner," said Elizabeth.

James Hutchings came out of his stupor.

"Why, L-L-Lizzie, you must let me p-p-put up our b-b-banns tomorrow," he stammered.

"Be off!" said Elizabeth, stamping her foot. "We can talk about that later."

When she came from her bath Olivia sent Elizabeth to tell Holloway that she would dine with Mr. Flexen and Mr. Manley that evening. She had a sudden desire to see more of Mr. Flexen, to weigh him as an antagonist.

Mr. Flexen was somewhat surprised to receive the information; then, considering the terms on which Olivia had been with her husband, he found her action natural enough. After all, she was not a woman of the middle class, bound to make a pretence of grieving for a wholly unamiable bully. Also, he was pleased: to dine with so charming a creature as Olivia would be pleasant and stimulating. In the course of the evening his wits might rise to the solution of his problem. Moreover, it would be odd if he did not gain a further, valuable insight into her character.

He was yet more surprised to find James Hutchings, still rather pale and haggard, but quite cool and master of himself, superintending the waiting of Wilkins and Holloway at dinner. Also, he liked the way in which he spoke to Olivia and looked at her. To Mr. Flexen, James Hutchings had the air of the authentic faithful dog. He was inclined to a better opinion of him.

Plainly, too, Olivia had learned that tongues were wagging against him, and had taken this way of checking them. It was a generous act. At the same time, he could very well believe that Olivia might, unconsciously of course, be on the side of the murderer of such a husband.

Thanks to Mr. Manley's invaluable sense of what was fitting, there was no constraint about the dinner. He had decided that they were three people of the world dining together, and the fact that there had been a murder in the house three days before and a funeral in the morning should not be allowed to impair their proper nonchalance. At the same time, decorum must be preserved; there must be no laughter.

Accordingly he took the conversation in hand, and kept it in hand. Mr. Flexen was somewhat astonished at the ability with which he did it; now and again he felt as if, personally, he were performing feats on the loose wire, but that, thanks to Mr. Manley, he was not going to fall off. They talked of the usual subjects on which people who have not a large circle of common acquaintances fall back. They all three abused the politicians with perfect sympathy; they abused the British drama with perfect sympathy; with no less perfect sympathy they abused the

Cubists and the Vorticists and the New Poets. Mr. Flexen had an odd feeling that they were behaving with entire naturalness and propriety; that their real interest was in the politicians, the British drama, the Cubists, the Vorticists and the New Poets, and not at all in the fate of the murderer of the late Lord Loudwater. After a while he found himself vying earnestly with Mr. Manley in an effort to display himself as a man of at least equal insight and intelligence.

Olivia did not talk much herself. She never did. But she displayed a quickness of understanding and soundness of judgment which stimulated them. All the while she was watching and weighing Mr. Flexen. He never once perceived it. Plainly enough, the talk did her good. She had come to dinner looking, Mr. Flexen thought, rather under the water. Before long she was looking, as she had resolved to look, her usual self. When, at a few minutes to nine, she left them, she was looking the most charming and sympathetic creature in the world, and, what was more, a creature without a care.

When the door closed behind her, she seemed to have taken with her a good deal of the brightness of the room. Mr. Flexen dropped back into his chair and frowned. In the silence which fell he wondered. Plainly she was free enough from care now.

"But when the feast is finished and the lamps expire-" Then Mr. Manley said, in a tone almost insolent: "If you think she murdered that red-eyed bull in a china shop, you're wrong. She didn't."

Mr. Flexen did not resent his tone. Indeed, before he could speak, it flashed on him that if she had done so, and Justice was depending on him himself to bring her to it, it was depending on a somewhat frail reed. He liked Mr. Manley for his readiness to fight for her cause.

He laughed gently and said: "I wasn't thinking so. I was only wondering." Then his eyes on Mr. Manley's face turned very keen, and he said: "I believe you know a good deal more about the affair than I do, if you liked to speak."

It seemed to him that for a moment Mr. Manley's desire to make himself valued struggled with his desire to be accurate.

Then the young man shook his head and said in a tone of surprise: "But what nonsense! You know so much more about it than I do. Why, you must have all the threads in your hands by now. I never even dreamt of the *Daily Wire's* mysterious woman."

"Not quite all—yet. But they're coming all right," said Mr. Flexen, with a confidence he was far from feeling.

James Hutchings, coming into the room to fetch cigarettes for Olivia, interrupted them.

"I'm glad to see you back again, Hutchings," said Mr. Manley in a tone of hearty congratulation. "Your going away for a trifle after all the years you've been here was a silly business."

"Thank you, sir," said Hutchings gratefully.

When Hutchings had gone, Mr. Flexen said: "It's all very well your talking, but it was you who suggested that Lady Loudwater was a woman of strong primitive emotions with a strain of Italian blood in her."

"I never suggested for a moment that she was a woman of *primitive* emotions," Mr. Manley protested with some vehemence.

"But the emotions of all women are primitive," said Mr. Flexen.

"Not the emotion excited in them by beauty," said Mr. Manley with chivalrous warmth. "And, hang it all! Does she look like a woman to commit murder?"

"Not on her own account, certainly," said Mr. Flexen.

"And on whose account should she commit murder?" cried Mr. Manley.

Mr. Flexen shrugged his shoulders.

"I said you knew ten times as much about the business as I do," said Mr. Manley in a tone of triumph.

14

Mr. Flexen awoke next morning hopeful of news of the mysterious woman. But the letters addressed to him at the Castle and those brought over from the office of the Chief Constable at Low Wycombe brought none. After breakfast, still hopeful, he telephoned to Scotland Yard. No information had reached it.

He perceived clearly that the case was at a deadlock till he had that information. He was sure that it would come sooner or later, possibly from the neighbourhood, more probably from London. It was always possible that Mr. Carrington might discover that some other lawyer had handled an entanglement for Lord Loudwater. In the meantime, his work at the Castle was done. He had exhausted its possibilities. There was no reason why he should not return to his rooms at Low Wycombe. After having conferred with Inspector Perkins, he decided to leave one of the two detectives to continue making inquiries in the neighbourhood. He told James Hutchings that he would like his clothes packed, and went to the rose-garden to taken his leave of Olivia and thank her for her hospitality.

He found her looking very charming in a light summer frock of white lace with a few black bows set about it, and he thought that she seemed less under a strain than she had seemed the day before. He told her that he was returning to Low Wycombe; she expressed regret at his going, and thanked him for his efforts to clear up the matter of Lord Loudwater's death. They parted on the friendliest terms.

As he came away, Mr. Flexen thought it significant that, though she had thanked him for his efforts, she had made no inquiry about the result of them. It might be that she dreaded to hear that they were on the way to be successful.

He observed that James Hutchings, who watched over his actual departure, seemed less pale and haggard than he had been the night before. He could well believe that he was glad to see him going without having had him arrested.

As he drove through the park he told himself that Lady Loudwater and Mr. Manley between them would probably break down any case the police might bring against anyone but the mysterious woman, and they might break down that. For his part, he was not going to give much time or attention to it till the mysterious woman had been discovered, and he did not think that he would be urged by Headquarters to do so after he had sent in his report, for, mindful of what he had told them of the unsatisfactory nature of Dr. Thornhill's evidence, Mr. Gregg in the *Daily Wire* and Mr. Douglas on the *Daily Planet* were dealing with the case in a half-hearted manner, though they were still clamouring with some vivacity for the mysterious woman.

As Mr. Flexen came out of the park gates he met William Roper on the edge of the West wood, stopped the car, and walked a few yards down the road to talk to him out of hearing of the chauffeur.

"I gather that you haven't told anyone of what you saw on the night of Lord Loudwater's death; or I should have heard of it," he said.

"Not a word, I haven't," said William Roper.

"That's good," said Mr. Flexen in a tone of warm approval. "It might spoil everything to put people on their guard."

He was more strongly than ever resolved to prevent, if he could, the gamekeeper from setting afoot a scandal about Lady Loudwater which could be of no service to the police or anyone else.

"Everybody says as James Hutchings did it, sir," said William Roper.

"H'm! And what do they say about the mysterious lady the papers are talking about–the lady you saw?"

"Oh, they don't pay no 'eed to 'er–not about 'ere, sir. They know Jim Hutchings," said William Roper contemptuously.

"I see," said Mr. Flexen.

"'Er ladyship and Colonel Grey, they still spends a lot of their time in the East wood pavilion. But now 'er ladyship's a widder, it's nobody's business but their own, I reckon," said William Roper.

"Of course not, of course not," said Mr. Flexen quickly, pleased to find that the ferret-faced gamekeeper attached so little importance to it. "I suppose people about here see that."

"They don't know about it. Nobody knows about it but me, and I don't tell everything I sees unless there's something to be got by it. A still tongue makes a wise 'ead, I say," said William Roper, with a somewhat vainglorious air.

"Quite right–quite right," said Mr. Flexen heartily. "Many a man's tongue has lost him a good job."

"You're right there, sir. But not me it won't," said William Roper with emphasis.

"I can see that. You've too much sense. Well, I shall keep in touch with you, and when the time comes you'll be called on. Drink my health. Good day," said Mr. Flexen, giving him half-a-crown.

He walked back to the car, pleased to have done Olivia the service of closing William Roper's mouth, at any rate for a time. He would talk, of course, sooner or later, probably sooner. But he might have closed his mouth for a fortnight.

William Roper walked on to the village and went into the "Bull and Gate." The village was simmering in a very lively fashion. The return of James Hutchings to his situation at the Castle was a fact with which it could not grapple easily. It was bewildered and annoyed.

William Roper had not, as he had assured Mr. Flexen, told what he had seen on the night of the murder of Lord Loudwater, but he had been dropping hints. He dropped more. He was a supporter of the theory that James Hutchings was the murderer because he desired to oust the father of James Hutchings from his post as head-gamekeeper. That was the reason also of his belief in James Hutchings' guilt. He was beginning to enjoy the interest he awakened as the storehouse of undivulged knowledge. When Mr. Flexen had supposed that he would remain silent for a fortnight, he had overestimated both his modesty and his reticence.

Later in the day the village was further upset by the behaviour of James Hutchings himself. He came into the "Bull and Gate" with an easy air, showed himself but little more civil than usual, and told the landlord that he had just arranged that the parson should publish the banns of his marriage with Elizabeth Twitcher on the following Sunday. The village was staggered. This was not the way in which it expected a man who would presently be tried and hanged for murder to behave.

In all fairness to James Hutchings, it must be said that he would not have acted with this decision of his own accord. Elizabeth had bidden him to it, urging that a bold front was half the battle. However grave her own doubts of his innocence might be, she was resolved that such doubts should, if possible, be banished from the minds of other people. Under her influence he was already becoming his old self as far as looks went. A shade of his usual ruddiness had come back; he was losing his haggardness.

With the going of Mr. Flexen there came a lull. His departure was a relief to Olivia, to Colonel Grey, and to James Hutchings. Doubtless he was still working on the case; but, working at a distance, he seemed less of a menace. All three of them seemed less under a strain.

Olivia and Grey spent their hours together in a less feverish eagerness to make the most of them.

Even Helena Truslove, when Mr. Manley told her that Mr. Flexen had left the Castle, said that she was very pleased to hear it. She looked very pleased. Mr. Manley's sense of what was fitting restrained him from asking her the reason of this pleasure. He had, indeed, no great desire to hear the reason of it from her own lips. It was enough for him to guess that she was the mysterious woman. He felt no need of her full confidence.

The Castle seemed to be settling down to its old round, the quieter for the loss of Lord Loudwater. His heir in Mesopotamia had been informed of his death by cable. But no cable in reply had come from him. Mr. Manley remained at the Castle as secretary to Olivia, who was making preparations leisurely to leave it and settle down in a flat in London. Colonel Grey was recovering from his wound with a passable quickness. James Hutchings had come to look very much his old self. Thanks to the shock he had had and thanks to Elizabeth, he wore a more subdued air, and was much more amiable with his fellow-servants.

The *Daily Wire*, the *Daily Planet*, and the rest of the newspapers had let the Loudwater mystery slip quietly out of their columns. Mr. Flexen was waiting with quiet expectation for information about the unknown woman. Since the advertisement the papers had given her had failed to produce that information he had a London detective working on the life in London, before his marriage, of the murdered man. Mr. Carrington had found nothing among Lord Loudwater's papers in the office of his firm to throw any light on the matter.

The chief actors in the affair regarded the quiet turn it had taken with a timorous satisfaction. Not so William Roper; William Roper was thoroughly dissatisfied. He had been willing enough to hold his tongue, because by so doing his unexpected and damning appearance at the trial would be the more dramatic and impressive. But he was impatient to make that appearance, and chafed at the delay. Also, his prestige was waning. The village was losing interest in the mystery, and it no longer looked to him to drop hints as the holder of the secret. That did not prevent him from dropping them. He would bring up the subject of the murder in order to drop them. His acquaintances who wished now to talk about other things found this practice tiresome. They did not hide this feeling. Matters came to a climax one evening in the bar of the "Bull and Gate."

William Roper dragged the subject of the murder into a conversation on the high price of groceries, and then, as usual, hinted at the things he could say and he would.

John Pittaway, who had been leading the conversation about the high price of groceries, turned on him and said with asperity: "I don't believe as there's anything you can tell us as we don't know, or you'd 'ave told it afore this fast enough, William Roper."

"That's what I've been thinking this long time," said old Bob Carter, who had for over forty years made a point of agreeing with the most disagreeable person at the moment in the bar of the "Bull and Gate."

"Isn't there? You wait an' see. You wait till the trial," said William Roper.

"Trial? There won't be no trial. 'Oo's a goin' to be tried? They ain't agoin' to try Jim 'Utchings. It's plain that 'er ladyship 'as set 'er face against that. And, wot's more, they can't 'ave much to try 'im on, or they'd 'ave to do it, in spite o' wot she said," said John Pittaway in yet more disagreeable accents.

William Roper was very angry. This was not to be borne. Indeed, if John Pittaway were right, and there was to be no trial, where was his dramatic and impressive appearance at it? He had better be dramatic and impressive now.

"Who said as they were goin' to try Jim 'Utchings? I never did," he growled. "There was other people went to the Castle that night besides Jim 'Utchings, and that mysterierse woman the papers talked about."

"An' 'ow do you know?" said John Pittaway in a tone of most disagreeable incredulity.

"I know because I seed 'em," said William Roper.

"Saw 'oo?" said John Pittaway.

Then the whole story he had told Mr. Flexen burst forth from William Roper's overcharged bosom, the story with the embellishments natural to the lapse of time since its first telling. No less naturally in the course of the discussion which followed, he told also the story of the luckless kiss in the East wood, and the landlord pounced on that as the cause of the quarrel between Lord Loudwater and Colonel Grey at Bellingham. William Roper supported his contention with an embellished account of the interview with Lord Loudwater in which he had informed him of that kiss.

It was, indeed, his great hour, not as great as the hour he had promised himself at the trial, not so public, but a great hour.

He left the "Bull and Gate" at closing time that night a man, in the estimation of all there, whose evidence could hang four of his fellow-creatures, the great man of the village.

Next morning the village was indeed simmering, and the scandal rose and spread from it like a stench. That very afternoon Mr. Manley heard it from Helena Truslove, and the next morning Mr. Flexen received two anonymous letters conveying the information to him, and suggesting that Colonel Grey and the Lady Loudwater had between them made away with her husband. It is hard to say whether Mr. Manley or Mr. Flexen was more annoyed by William Roper's blabbing.

But there was nothing to be done. The scandal must run its course. Mr. Flexen did not think that it would find its way into the papers, local or London. None the less, he was alive to the danger that a sudden heavy pressure might be put on the police, and he might be forced to take ill-advised action, start a prosecution which would do Lady Loudwater infinite harm, and yet end in a fiasco which would leave the mystery just where it was. The one bright spot in the affair was that Lord Loudwater appeared to have left no friends behind him who would make it their business to see that he was avenged. As long as that avenging was everybody's business it was nobody's business.

Elizabeth Twitcher was no less disturbed than Mr. Flexen. She felt that Olivia ought to be informed of what was being said that she might be able to take steps to meet the danger. She took counsel with James Hutchings, who could not help feeling relieved by this diversion of suspicion, and he agreed with her that Olivia should be informed of the scandal at once. But it was an uncommonly unpleasant task, and she shrank from it.

Then a happy thought came to James Hutchings, and he said: "Look here: let Mr. Manley do it. He's her ladyship's secretary, and it's the kind of thing he'll do very well. He's a tactful young fellow."

"It would be a blessing if he did," said Elizabeth with a sigh. She paused and added: "You do speak differently about him to what you used to."

"Yes. I made a mistake about him like as I did about some other people," said James Hutchings, with a rather shame-faced air. "He behaved very well about seeing me here the night the master was murdered and saying nothing to the police about it. An' then he congratulated me very handsomelike on coming back as butler before Mr. Flexen."

"He would do it better than I should," said Elizabeth.

"Then I'll speak to him about it," said James Hutchings.

He paused a while to kiss Elizabeth, then went in search of Mr. Manley. He learned from Holloway that he had come in about twenty minutes earlier and was in his sitting-room. He went to him and found him looking through the MS. of the play he was writing, with an unlighted pipe in his mouth.

"If you please, sir, I thought I'd better come and tell you that they're saying in the village that Colonel Grey kissed her ladyship in the East wood on the afternoon of his lordship's death, and his lordship was informed of it and quarrelled with Colonel Grey and then her ladyship, and she and Colonel Grey made away with his lordship," said James Hutchings.

"I've heard something about it," said Mr. Manley, frowning, and he struck a match. "Who set this absurd story going?"

"William Roper, one of the under-gamekeepers, sir."

"William Roper? Ah, I know—a ferret-faced young fellow."

"Yes, sir. And we was thinking that her ladyship ought to know about it so as she can put a stop to it at once, and you were the proper person to tell her, sir," said James Hutchings.

On the instant Mr. Manley saw himself discharging this unpleasant but important duty with intelligence and tact, and he said readily: "I was thinking of doing so, and now that I know the lying rascal's name I can do it at once. The sooner this kind of thing is stopped the better."

"Thank you, sir," said Hutchings, and with a sigh of relief he left the room.

He had reached the top of the stairs when the door of Mr. Manley's room opened; he appeared on the threshold and said: "Will you send someone to tell William Roper to be here at nine o'clock tonight? And it wouldn't be a bad idea to drop a hint to anyone you send that William Roper has got himself into serious trouble."

Mr. Manley thought quickly.

"Very good, sir," said James Hutchings, and he hurried down the stairs. Mr. Manley did not see Olivia at once, for she was still in the pavilion in the East wood. But as soon as she returned, he sent a message by

Holloway to her, that he wished to see her on important business. Holloway brought word that she would see him at once.

He found her in her sitting-room, gazing out of the window, and she turned quickly at his entrance with inquiring eyes.

"It's a rather unpleasant business, and the sooner it's dealt with the better," said Mr. Manley in a brisk, businesslike voice. "One of the under-gamekeepers has been spreading a scandalous and lying story about you and Colonel Grey, something about his kissing you in the East wood on the afternoon of Lord Loudwater's death, and he has gone on to suggest, or assert–I don't know which–that you and Colonel Grey had a hand in Lord Loudwater's death."

The blow she had been expecting had fallen, and Olivia paled and her mouth went dry.

"Which of the under-gamekeepers is it?" she said calmly but with difficulty, for her tongue kept sticking to the roof of her mouth.

"A ferret-faced, rascally-looking fellow, called William Roper," said Mr. Manley with some heat. Then, to save her the effort of speaking, he went on: "Of course you'd like him discharged at once. The sooner these people understand that their excitement about Lord Loudwater's death is not going to be held an excuse for telling lying stories the better. You will not be troubled by any more of them."

Olivia looked at him with steady eyes. She had recovered herself and was thinking hard. Mr. Manley's certainty about the right method of dealing with the matter was catching. It was better to show a bold front and at once. There was no time to consult Antony Grey.

"Yes. You're quite right, Mr. Manley. Gentle measures are of no use with this kind of scandal-monger. William Roper must be discharged at once," she said quietly.

"Perhaps you would like me to deal with him? It's rather a business for a man," Mr. Manley suggested.

"Yes, if you would," she said in a grateful tone.

"I will, as soon as I can get hold of him," said Mr. Manley cheerfully. "He'll make no more mischief about here," He went out of the room briskly.

His confidence was heartening. When the door closed behind him Olivia sobbed twice in the reaction from the shock of his announcement. Then she recovered herself and went quietly to her bath. She observed Elizabeth's sympathetic manner as she dressed her hair. Evidently all the servants as well as the villagers were talking about her. But for its possible, dangerous consequences, she was indifferent to their talk. She was now wholly absorbed in Grey; he was the only thing of any importance in her life.

Mr. Manley ate his dinner with an excellent appetite. He was pleased with the brisk, almost brusque, manner in which he had dealt with the matter of William Roper, in his interview with Olivia. If he had shilly-shallied and hummed and hawed about the scandal, it would have been so much more unpleasant for her. He thought, too, that his practical, common-sense attitude to the business would probably help her to take it more easily, and he was sure that he had advised the best measure to be taken with William Roper.

He was smoking a cigar in a great content, when at nine o'clock Holloway brought him word that William Roper had come. Mr. Manley bade him bring him to him at a quarter-past. He felt that suspense would make William Roper malleable, and he intended to hammer him. At thirteen minutes past nine he composed his face into a dour truculence, an expression to which the heavy conformation of the lower part lent itself admirably.

William Roper, looking uncommonly ill at ease, was ushered in by James Hutchings himself, and the butler had improved the thirteen shining minutes he had had with him by increasing to a considerable degree his uneasiness and anxiety.

Mr. Manley did not greet William Roper. He stood on the hearth-rug and glowered at him with heavy truculence. William Roper shuffled his feet and fumbled with his cap.

Then Mr. Manley said: "Her ladyship has been informed that you have been spreading scandalous reports in the village, and she has instructed me to discharge you at once." He walked across to the table, took the sheet of notepaper on which he had written the amount due to William Roper, dipped a pen in the ink, and added: "Here are your wages up to date, and a week's wages in lieu of notice. Sign this receipt."

He dipped a pen in the ink and held it out to William Roper with very much the air of Lady Macbeth presenting her husband with the dagger.

William Roper was stupefied. Mr. Manley, truculent and dramatic, cowed him.

"I never done nothing, sir," he said feebly.

"Sign—at once!" said Mr. Manley, gazing at him with the glare of the basilisk.

"I ain't agoing to sign. I ain't done nothing to be discharged. I ain't said nothing but what I seed with my own eyes," William Roper protested.

"Sign!" said Mr. Manley, tapping the receipt like an official in a spy play. "Sign!"

He was too much for William Roper. The conflict, such as it was, of wills ceased abruptly. William Roper signed.

Mr. Manley pushed the money towards him as towards a loathed pariah. William Roper counted it, and put it in his pocket. He walked towards the door with an air of stupefied dejection.

"Also, you are to be off the estate by twelve o'clock tomorrow. Loudwater is not the place for ungrateful and slanderous rogues," said Mr. Manley.

William Roper stopped and turned; his face was working malignantly.

"We'll see what Mr. Flexen's got to say about this," he snarled, went through the door, and slammed it behind him.

15

Olivia came that night to her tryst with Grey in a great dejection. She perceived clearly enough that the instant discharge of William Roper would not stop the scandal, and she was desperately afraid of the results of it. The hope which had sprung up in her mind on reading in the *Daily Wire* the story of her husband's quarrel with an unknown woman died down. This was a far more important matter, and she could not see how the police could fail to act on William Roper's story.

She found Grey waiting for her with his wonted impatience, and presently told him about William Roper.

"This is the very thing I've been fearing," he said with a sudden heaviness.

"It will certainly force Mr. Flexen's hand," she said.

"I don't know—I don't know," he said more hopefully. "Flexen struck me as being the kind of man to act just when it suited him, and I expect that he had known all along anything William Roper had to tell."

"Yes, he did. Twitcher told me that Roper had an interview with him on the afternoon after Egbert's death," she said, catching a little of his hopefulness.

"Well, if he hasn't done anything about it so far, there's no reason why he should act immediately the story becomes common property," he said in a tone of relief.

"No—no," she said slowly. Then she sobbed once and cried: "But, oh, this waiting's so dreadful! Never knowing what's going to happen and when—feeling that he's lying in wait all the time."

"It is pretty awful," he said, drawing her more closely to him and kissing her.

She clung tightly to him, quivering.

"The only thing to do is to stick it out, and when the time comes–if it comes–put up a good fight. I think we shall," he said in a cheering tone.

"Of course we will," she said firmly, gave herself a little shake, and relaxed her grip a little.

He kissed her again, and they were silent a while, both of them thinking hard.

Then he said: "Look here: let's get married."

"Get married?" she said.

"Yes. The more we belong to one another the better we shall feel."

"But–but won't there be rather an outcry at our marrying so soon?" she said.

"Oh, if people knew of it, yes. But I don't propose that they should. We'll get married quite quietly. I'll get a special licence. The padre of my regiment is in Town, and he'll marry us. I can find a couple of witnesses who'll hold their tongues. We can get married in twenty-four hours. Will you?"

"Yes," she said firmly.

His surprise at her ready assent was drowned in the joy it gave him.

The next morning at half-past nine Mr. Manley rang up Mr. Flexen at his office at Low Wycombe.

When he heard his voice he said: "Good morning, Flexen. A young fellow of the name of William Roper will be calling on you this morning. I expect you know all he has to say already. But do you see anything to be gained by his making a pestiferous, scandal-mongering nuisance of himself?"

"I do not. I will say a few kind words to him," said Mr. Flexen grimly.

Mr. Manley thanked him and rang off. Then he sent Hutchings down to the village to let it be known that anyone who let William Roper lodge in his or her cottage would at once receive notice to quit it. He thought it improbable, in view of the general unpleasantness of

William Roper, that he would be called on to carry out the threat.

William Roper had already started to pay his visit to Mr. Flexen. Mr. Flexen kept him dangling his heels in his office for three-quarters of an hour before he saw him. This cold welcome allowed much of William Roper's sense of his great importance in the district to ooze out of him.

Mr. Flexen emptied him of the rest of it. He greeted him curtly, heard his story with a deepening frown, and abused him at some length for a babbling idiot, and sent him about his business. William Roper returned to his mother's cottage to find that her only object in life was to get him out of her cottage then and there. She had conceived the idea that the whole affair was a plot to have a good excuse for giving her notice to leave that cottage. She knew well that it was the opinion of all its other inhabitants that the village would be much better without her and that there were very good grounds for it.

William Roper perceived with uncommon clearness the truth of Mr. Flexen's assertion that he was a babbling idiot. His dream of outing William Hutchings from the post of head-gamekeeper and filling it himself was forever shattered, and he had been the great man of the village for little more than fourteen hours, ten of which he had spent in sleep. He cursed the hour in which he had espied that luckless kiss, and too late perceived the folly of a humble gamekeeper's meddling with the affairs of those who own the game he keeps.

The next morning Elizabeth observed that her mistress was another creature, almost her old self indeed. The air of strain and oppression had, for the time being at any rate, gone from her face. She moved with her old alertness. She even smiled at Elizabeth's strictures on the treacherous William Roper.

After breakfast she bade Elizabeth pack a trunk for her, since she was going to London that afternoon and would spend the night, perhaps two or three days, there.

Also, she chose, with frowning thoughtfulness and no little changing of mind, the frocks she would take with her, and discussed carefully with Elizabeth the changes necessary to give them a sufficiently mourning character.

Elizabeth was indeed pleased with the change in her mistress. She ascribed it to the influence of Colonel Grey.

In the afternoon Olivia went to London and drove from Paddington to Grey's flat. She found him awaiting her with the most eager expectation. He had bought the special licence; the chaplain of his regiment and a wounded friend were coming at seven o'clock. After they were married, they would all four dine together, and, later, he and she would return to his flat.

They had tea, and then he showed her some of the beautiful things, for the most part ivory and jade, which were his most loved possessions. She admitted frankly that she had to learn to appreciate and admire them as they deserved. But she was sure that she would learn to do so.

She found the flat of a somewhat spartan simplicity after Loudwater Castle, Quainton Hall, and the houses to which she was used. But she also found that it had been furnished with a keen regard for comfort. In particular, she observed that the easy chairs, which were the chief furniture of the sitting-room, were the most comfortable she had ever taken her ease in.

At seven o'clock the padre and Sir Charles Ross, Grey's wounded friend, arrived. After they had talked for a few minutes, making Olivia's acquaintance, the padre married them. Henderson, Grey's valet, a tall, spare Scot with rugged features who in the course of his seven years' service had acquired, in his manner and way of speaking, a curious and striking likeness to his master, was the second witness.

It was wholly characteristic of Olivia that she felt no slightest need of the supporting presence of a woman. Yet, for all the unfamiliar simplicity of the scene, the ceremony did not lack dignity, or impressiveness. At the end of it Olivia felt herself very much more the wife of Antony Grey than she had ever felt herself the wife of Lord Loudwater.

They dined in a private dining-room at the "Ritz," and Olivia found the dinner delightful. The three men, after some desultory talk about common friends and the ordinary London subjects, fell to talking about their work and their fighting in France. She was most pleased by the evident respect and admiration with which the other two regarded her husband. It was a new experience for her to be married to a man for whom anyone showed respect.

At a few minutes past ten she and Grey went home to his flat. They preferred to walk.

Olivia did not return to Loudwater for three days. Grey did not return till the day after that. Then they again spent much of their time in the pavilion in the East wood, and since Olivia was careful not to replace William Roper, no one knew of their meetings. Every week they went to London for two days. They lived in an absorption in one another which left them little time to be troubled by fears of the danger which hung over them. The scandal about them ran the usual nine days' course. Then, since no new development of the Loudwater case arose to give it a fresh, active life, it died down.

About a fortnight after their marriage Mr. Manley retired from his post of secretary and went to London. A few days later he married Helena Truslove at the office of a registrar, and they established themselves in a furnished flat at Clarence Gate, while they furnished a flat of their own. Mr. Manley found himself, under the influence of domesticity, the stimulation of life in London, and the society of the intelligent, writing his new play with all the ease and vigour he had expected.

Mr. Flexen was beginning, somewhat gloomily, to think it probable that the problem of the death of Lord Loudwater would have to be set among the unsolved problems which have at different times baffled the police.

Then, before he had quite lost hope, there came a letter from Mr. Carrington. It ran:

"Dear Mr. Flexen,

"I received this morning a letter from Mrs. Marshall, of 3, Laburnum Terrace, Low Wycombe, asking me, as the agent of the present Lord Loudwater, to have some repairs made to the house in which she is his lordship's tenant. We have never handled this property; we did not even know that it belonged to the late Lord Loudwater. If you can find the man who managed it for him, he may be able to give you the information you want.

"Yours faithfully,

"C.R.W. CARRINGTON."

In ten minutes Mr. Flexen was at 3, Laburnum Terrace; in a quarter of an hour he had learned that Mrs. Marshall had paid her rent to Mr. Shepherd, of 9, Bolton Street, Low Wycombe; in twenty minutes he had learned from Mrs. Shepherd that her husband was in Mesopotamia, and that she had not heard from him for two months. In half an hour from the time he read Mr. Carrington's letter he was in the train on his way to London. To get in touch with Captain Shepherd in that distant and backward land was a matter for Scotland Yard. No acting Chief Constable would do so without considerable delay.

He drafted the telegram in consultation with one of the commissioners, who himself set about the business of getting it through to Captain Shepherd and receiving his answer to it. Then he returned to Low Wycombe. Three days later came a letter from Scotland Yard to inform him that Captain Shepherd was in an out-of-the-way district in the north of Mesopotamia, and that there must be a delay of days before he received the telegram and sent his answer to it. Mr. Flexen possessed his soul in the patience of a man who was sure that he was going to get what he wanted.

A few days later, on a Saturday, his work took him to Loudwater, and he called on Olivia. He found her a different creature. She had lost her air of being under a strain, and save that her eyes were at first anxious, she showed herself wholly at her ease with him. He came away assuring himself that she was one of the most charming women he had ever met. He took it that she still met Colonel Grey in the pavilion in the East wood, and that after a decorous lapse of time they would marry. He thought Colonel Grey uncommonly fortunate.

Then he again wondered what had so perturbed them when he had been at the Castle inquiring into the death of Lord Loudwater. What did they know of the mystery? What part had they played in it?

Soon after he had left her Olivia went to London to spend the week-end with her husband. But she did not go in her wonted joyful mood. She tried to thrust it out of her mind; but Mr. Flexen's visit had brought back her old fear. Grey at once perceived that she was not in good spirits, and he was a little alarmed. He had firmly kept his thought from the danger which still hung over them. Now he caught from her something of her uneasiness. But he would not yield to it, and by the end of dinner he had, for the while at any rate, banished it from both their minds.

Then when he awoke that night, quietly, at the turning hour, he heard Olivia crying very softly.

He put his arm round her and said seriously "What is it, darling? What's the matter?"

"Oh, why ever did you kill him?" she wailed. "He–he wasn't worth it. And I'd have come to you without. And we might have been so happy!"

Grey, with a start, sat bolt upright, and in a tone of the last astonishment stammered: "K-K-Kill him? Me? B-B-But I thought you k-k-killed him!"

He had never been so taken aback in his life.

Olivia sat bolt upright in her turn.

"Me?" she said in an astonishment fully as great as his. "No, I didn't."

Then with one accord they clung to one another and laughed tremulously in an immeasurable relief.

Then Olivia said: "And you didn't mind? You married me when you actually thought I'd murdered Egbert?"

"Oh, Egbert!" said Grey in a tone of contempt which placed the late Lord Loudwater definitely as a person the murder of whom was neither here nor there. Then he added: "But, hang it all! You married me when you actually thought I'd murdered him."

"I thought you did it for my sake," said Olivia.

"I thought you did it for mine—to get me out of a mess. Though I'll be shot if I believe I should have cared if you'd done it entirely on your own account. Not that you could."

"Oh, Antony, how very fond of one another we must be!" said Olivia in a hushed voice.

It was after breakfast next morning that Olivia, who stood before the window, smoking a cigarette and watching the passers-by, turned and said: "But if neither you nor I murdered Egbert, who did?"

"The mysterious woman, I suppose," said Grey, with very little show of interest in the matter.

"But I never believed that there was any mysterious woman, I thought the papers invented her," said Olivia.

"So did I," said Grey. "But it's beginning to look to me as if there might have been one."

"I wonder who she can be?" said Olivia.

"A barmaid, I should think," said Grey, in a tone which placed definitely the late Lord Loudwater as a lover.

"You certainly do dislike Egbert," said Olivia, in a dispassionate tone of one stating a natural fact of little importance.

"I do," said Grey.

"It's odd how little I remember him," said Olivia thoughtfully. "But then I was always trying to forget him unless he was actually in the room with me. And then I was always trying not to see him."

"I remember the way he treated you," said Grey sternly.

Olivia smiled at him.

"I hope to goodness the police never do find that wretched woman!" he said.

Olivia frowned thoughtfully. Then she smiled again.

"I don't think it would be much use if they did," she said. "I told Mr. Flexen that I heard Egbert snoring about twelve o'clock. I didn't; but I thought that as you went away about half-past eleven, it would make it safer for you. I could always stick to it, if we thought it right."

"And I told Flexen that I didn't hear him snoring at about half-past eleven, and I did. I thought it would make it safer for you."

"Well, we are—" said Olivia, and she laughed.

Then of a sudden her eyes sparkled and she cried: "But if you heard him snore at half-past eleven that lets the mysterious woman out. She went away at a quarter-past."

"By Jove! So it does," said Grey.

Three days later, driving back in the evening from Rickmansworth to Low Wycombe, Mr. Flexen passed Grey on his way home from an afternoon's fishing. He stopped the car, and as Grey came up to it he perceived that he was looking uncommonly well, though his limp appeared to be as bad as ever. He was not only looking well, he was also looking happy, wholly free from care.

They greeted one another and Mr. Flexen said: "By Jove! You are looking fit!"

"Yes, I'm all right again," said Grey. Then he frowned and added: "But the nuisance of it is that I shall always have this confounded limp."

"You get off more lightly than a good many men I know," said Flexen sadly.

"Yes. I'm not grousing much," said Grey.

There came a pause, and then Grey said: "I've been rather hoping to come across you. When you questioned me about my doings on the night of Loudwater's death, you asked me whether I heard him snore as I went through the library, going in and out of the Castle, and for reasons which seemed quite good to me at the time I told you I didn't. As a matter of fact, he was snoring like a pig when I came out."

Mr. Flexen looked at him hard, thinking quickly. Then he said softly: "My goodness! That would be half-past eleven!"

"Close on it," said Grey.

"Well as a matter of fact, I didn't believe you," said Mr. Flexen frankly. "In my business, you know, one acquires a very good ear for the truth."

Grey laughed cheerfully and said: "I expect you do."

"All the same, I'm glad to have it for certain," said Mr. Flexen, smiling at him. "Well, I must be getting on; let me give you a lift as far as Loudwater."

Grey thanked him and stepped into the car.

When he had set him down, Mr. Flexen drove on in frowning thought. Colonel Grey was speaking the truth, and in that case neither James Hutchings nor the mysterious woman had committed the murder, unless they had deliberately returned for the purpose. He did not believe that James Hutchings had returned; he thought it improbable that the mysterious woman had returned.

Even more important was the fact that this admission of Colonel Grey assured him that neither he nor Lady Loudwater had committed the murder. Grey had evidently lied to shield her. He had no less evidently learned that she did not need shielding. That admission had not at all simplified the problem.

The next morning Scotland Yard telegraphed to him the reply to its cable to Captain Shepherd. It ran:

Loudwater allowed Mrs. Helena Truslove Crest Loudwater six hundred a year and gave her Crest.

He had the mysterious woman at last!

He drove over to the Crest at once and learned from the caretaker that Mrs. Truslove was now living in London in a flat at Clarence Gate. He could not get away from his work till the afternoon, and it was past half-past four when he knocked at the door of her flat.

The maid led him down the passage, opened the door on the right, and announced him.

Helena was sitting beside a table on which afternoon tea for two was set. She looked surprised to hear his name.

"Mrs. Truslove?" he said.

"I was Mrs. Truslove," she said, rising and holding out her hand. "But now I am Mrs. Manley. You know my husband. He will be so pleased to see you again. I'm expecting him every minute."

Mr. Flexen was for a moment conscious of a slight sensation of vertigo. The mysterious woman was the wife of Herbert Manley!

He could not at once see the bearings of this fact, but ideas, fancies and suspicions raced one another through his head.

He checked them and said in a somewhat toneless voice: "I shall be delighted to see him again. Have you been married long?"

"Rather more than a fortnight." said Helena. "But do sit down. My husband will be so pleased to see you again. He has a great admiration for you."

Mr. Flexen sat down and unconsciously stared hard at her. Ideas were jostling one another in his head.

"We won't wait for him. I'll have the tea made at once," she said, bending forward to press the bell-button.

"One moment, please," he said in his crispest, most official voice. "I've come to see you on a very important matter."

"Oh?" she said quickly, frowning. Then she looked at him with steady eyes.

"Yes. You know that I am investigating the Loudwater case, and I have received information that you are the mysterious lady who visited Lord Loudwater on the night of his death and had a violent quarrel with him."

"We began by quarrelling," she said quietly.

"*Began* by quarrelling?" said Mr. Flexen.

"Yes. I'd better tell you the whole story, and you'll understand," she said in a matter-of-fact voice. "Rather more than two years ago I was engaged to be married to Lord Loudwater. He broke off our engagement and married Miss Quainton. I was not going to stand that, and I was going to bring a breach of promise action against him. He didn't want that, of course. It would most likely have stopped his marrying Miss Quainton. So he agreed to make over the Crest, my house just beyond Loudwater, to me, and pay me an allowance of six hundred a year."

"This was two years ago?" said Mr. Flexen.

"Yes," said Helena. "But stupidly, though I had the house properly made over to me, I didn't have a deed about the allowance. And a few days before he committed suicide–"

"Committed suicide?" Mr. Flexen interrupted.

"Of course he committed suicide. Didn't Dr. Thornhill say that the wound might have been self-inflicted? Besides, poor Egbert had a most frightful temper."

"But why should he commit suicide?" said Mr. Flexen.

"He may have been upset about Lady Loudwater and Colonel Grey. Why, I'm quite sure that it would drive him mad–absolutely mad for the time being. I know him well enough to be sure of that."

"Yes–yes," said Mr. Flexen slowly. "It's a tenable theory, doubtless. But about your quarrel with him."

"A few days before he died he talked about halving my allowance. And, of course, I was frightfully annoyed about it. I wanted to have it out with him–I meant to–but I knew that he'd never let me get near him, if he could help it. But I knew, too, that he sat in the smoking-room every evening after dinner, and generally went to sleep. You know everything about everyone in the country, you know. And I determined to take him by surprise, and I did. We did have a row, for I was frightfully angry. It seemed so mean. But he stopped it by telling me that he had instructed his bankers—we have the same bankers—to pay twelve thousand pounds into my account instead of allowing me six hundred a year."

There was just the faintest change in her voice as she spoke the last sentence, and it did not escape Mr. Flexen's sensitive ear. He thought that the whole story had been rehearsed; it sounded so. But she spoke the last sentence just a little more quickly. The rest of the story rang true, or, at any rate, truer.

"Twelve thousand pounds," he said slowly. "And did Lord Loudwater tell you when he instructed his bankers?"

"No. But it must have been that very day. The letter must have been in the post, in fact, for two mornings later I received a letter from the bank telling me that they had credited me with that amount—the morning after the inquest, I think it was."

"I see," said Mr. Flexen, and he paused, considering the story. Then he said: "And were you surprised at all at his doing this?"

"Yes, I was," she said frankly. "It didn't seem like him. But since I've wondered whether he had made up his mind to commit suicide and wished to leave things quite straight."

It was a plausible theory, but Mr. Flexen did not believe that Lord Loudwater had committed suicide.

"I suppose that your husband knows all about it?" he said at random.

"He may, and he may not. He hasn't said anything to me about it," she said.

"Then we may take it that he did not write the letter of instruction to the bankers," said Mr. Flexen.

"Oh, he might have done and still have said nothing about it. He has a very sensitive delicacy and might have thought it my business and not his. I haven't told him about the twelve thousand pounds yet. I don't bother him about business matters. In fact, I'm going to manage his business as well as my own."

"And he didn't know about the allowance?" said Mr. Flexen.

"Oh, yes, he did. I told him all about that," said Helena quickly.

Mr. Flexen paused, considering. He seemed to have learnt from her all she had to tell.

There came the sound of the opening of the door of the flat and of steps in the hall. Then the door of the room opened, and Mr. Manley came in. Mr. Flexen's eyes swept over him. He was looking cheerful, prosperous, and rather sleek. His air had grown even more important and assured.

He greeted Mr. Flexen warmly and beamed on him. Then he demanded tea. But Mr. Flexen rose, declared that he must be going, and in spite of Mr. Manley's protests went. It had flashed on him that he might just catch Mr. Carrington at his office.

16

Mr. Flexen did find Mr. Carrington at his office, and Mr. Carrington's first words were:

"Well, have you found the mysterious woman?"

"I've found the mysterious woman, and she's now Mrs. Herbert Manley," said Mr. Flexen.

Mr. Carrington stared at him, then he said softly: "Well, I'm damned!"

"It does explain several things," said Mr. Flexen dryly. "We know now why she was so hard to find–why there was no trace of her relations with Lord Loudwater, no trace of Shepherd's managing the Low Wycombe property among his papers, why there were no pass-books."

Mr. Carrington flushed and said: "The young scoundrel had us on toast all the while."

"Toast is the word," said Mr. Flexen.

"I never did like the beggar. I couldn't stand his infernal manner. But it never occurred to me that he was a bad hat. I merely thought him a pretentious young ass who didn't know his place," said Mr. Carrington.

"I'm not so sure about the ass," said Mr. Flexen.

"No–perhaps not. He certainly brought it off for a time, and shielded her as long as it lasted," said Mr. Carrington slowly.

"She didn't need any shielding," said Mr. Flexen.

"Do you mean to tell me that she didn't murder Loudwater?"

"She did not. You don't murder a man who has just given you twelve thousand pounds," said Mr. Flexen.

"Twelve thousand pounds?" said Mr. Carrington slowly. Then he started from his chair and almost howled: "Are you telling me that Lord Loudwater gave this woman twelve thousand pounds! He never gave anyone twelve thousand pounds! He never gave anyone a thousand pounds! He never gave anyone fifty pounds! He couldn't have done it! Never in his life!"

His voice rose in a fine crescendo.

"Well, perhaps it was hardly a gift," said Mr. Flexen, and he told him Helena's story.

At the end of it Mr. Carrington said with dogged, sullen conviction: "I don't care, I don't believe it. Lord Loudwater couldn't have done it."

"But there's the letter from her bankers," said Mr. Flexen. "And I suppose you can trace the twelve thousand pounds."

Mr. Carrington started and said sharply: "Why, that must be where the rubber shares went to."

"What rubber shares?" said Mr. Flexen.

"We can't lay our hands on a block of rubber shares Lord Loudwater owned. The certificate isn't among his scrip—he kept all his scrip at the Castle—he wouldn't keep it at his bank. Those rubber shares were worth just about twelve thousand pounds."

"Well, there you are," said Mr. Flexen.

"No, I'm not, I tell you I don't believe in that gift—not even in the circumstances. Lord Loudwater would a thousand times rather have gone on paying the allowance—as little of it as he could. There's something fishy—very fishy—about it, I tell you," said Mr. Carrington vehemently.

"And where did the fishiness come in?" said Mr. Flexen.

Mr. Carrington was silent, frowning. Then he said: "I'll—I'll be hanged if I can see."

Mr. Flexen rose sharply and said: "There's only one point in the affair where it could have come in as far as I can see. I should like to examine Lord Loudwater's letter of instruction to his bankers."

"By George! You've got it," said Mr. Carrington.

"Well, can we get a look at it?" said Mr. Flexen.

"We can. Harrison, the manager, will stretch a point for me. He knows that I'm quite safe. Come along," said Mr. Carrington.

"At this hour? The bank's been closed this two hours," said Flexen.

"He'll be there. It's years since he got away before seven," said Mr. Carrington confidently.

He told a clerk to telephone to the bank that he was coming. They found a taxicab quickly, drove to the bank, entered it by the side door, and were taken straight to Mr. Harrison.

He made no bones about showing them Lord Loudwater's letter of instructions with regard to the twelve thousand pounds. Mr. Carrington and Mr. Flexen read it together. It was quite short, and ran:

"GENTLEMEN,

"I shall be much obliged by your paying the enclosed cheque from Messrs. Hanbury and Johnson for £12,046 into the account of Mrs. Helena Truslove.

"Yours faithfully,

"LOUDWATER."

"Rather a curt way of disposing of such a large sum," said Mr. Flexen, taking the letter and going to the window.

"It was the way Lord Loudwater did things," said Mr. Harrison.

"Yes, yes; I know," said Mr. Carrington. "Some things."

They both looked at Mr. Flexen, who was examining the letter through a magnifying glass.

He studied it for a good two minutes, turned to them with a quiet smile of triumph on his face and said: "I've never seen Lord Loudwater's signature. But this is a forgery."

"A forgery?" said the manager sharply, stepping quickly towards Mr. Flexen with outstretched hand.

"I'm not surprised to hear it," said Mr. Carrington.

"Well, the signature is not written with the natural ease with which a man signs his name," said Mr. Flexen, giving the letter to Mr. Harrison.

Mr. Harrison studied it carefully. Then he pressed a button on his desk and bade the clerk who came bring all the letters they had received from Lord Loudwater during the last three months of his life and bring them quickly.

Then he turned to Mr. Flexen and said stiffly: "I'm bound to say that the signature looks perfectly right to me."

"I've no doubt that it's a good forgery. It was done by a very clever man," said Mr. Flexen.

"A first-class young scoundrel," Mr. Carrington amended.

"We shall soon see," said Mr. Harrison, politely incredulous.

The clerk came with the letters. There were eight of them, all written by Mr. Manley and signed by Lord Loudwater.

The manager compared the signatures of every one of them with the signature in question, using a magnifying glass which lay on his desk.

Then, triumphant in his turn, he said curtly: "It's no forgery."

"Allow me," said Mr. Flexen, and in his turn he compared the signatures, again every one of them.

Then he said: "As I said, it's an uncommonly good forgery. You see that the bodies of the letters are all written with the same pen, a gold-nibbed fountain-pen; the signatures are written with a steel nib. It cuts deeper into the paper, and the ink doesn't flow off it so evenly. The forged signature is written with the same kind of nib as the genuine ones. Also, the bodies of the letters are written in a fountain-pen ink–the 'Swan,' I think. The signatures are written in Stephens' blue-black ink. The forged signature is also written in Stephens' blue-black ink. No error there, you see."

"You seem to know a good deal about these things," said Mr. Harrison, rather tartly.

"Yes. I've been a partner in Punchard's Agency–you know it; we've done some work for you–for the last two years. I didn't need this kind of knowledge for my work in India. I only made a special study of forgery after joining the agency. A private inquiry agency gets such a lot of it," said Mr. Flexen.

"Well, and if there's an error in these details, where is it? It's not in the signature itself," said Mr. Harrison.

"Indeed, it is," said Mr. Flexen. "It's an uncommonly good signature too. The 'Loud' is perfect. But the 'water' gives it away. The forger had evidently practised it a lot. In fact, he wrote the 'Loud' straight off. But the 'water' has no less than five distinct pauses in it–under the microscope, of course–where he paused to think, or perhaps to look at a genuine signature, the endorsement on the cheque very likely."

Mr. Harrison sniffed ever so faintly, and said: "Of course, I've had experience of handwriting experts–not very much, thank goodness!–and you differ among yourselves so. It's any odds that another expert will find those pauses in quite different places from you, or even no pauses at all."

Mr. Flexen laughed gently and said: "Perhaps. But he ought not to."

"There you are. And when it comes to a jury," said Mr. Harrison, and he threw out his hands. "Besides, if you got your experts to agree, you'd have to show a very strong motive."

"Oh, we've got that–we've got that," said Mr. Carrington with conviction.

"Well, of course that will make it easier for you to get the jury to believe your handwriting experts rather than those of the other side," said Mr. Harrison, without any enthusiasm. Then he added, with rather more cheerfulness: "But you never can tell with a jury."

"No; that's true," said Mr. Flexen quickly. "I'm sure we're very much obliged to you for showing us the letter."

There was nothing more to be done at the bank, and having again thanked Mr. Harrison, they took their leave of him. He showed no great cordiality in his leave-taking, he was looking at the matter from the point of view of the bank. The bank preferred to detect forgeries itself–in time.

As they came into the street, Mr. Carrington rubbed his hands together and said in a tone of deep satisfaction: "And now for the warrant."

"Warrant for whom?" said Mr. Flexen in a tone of polite inquiry.

"Manley. The sooner that young scoundrel is in gaol the better I shall feel," said Mr. Carrington.

"So should I," said Mr. Flexen. "But I'm very much afraid that for Mr. Manley it's a far cry to Holloway. We have no case against him whatever–not a scrap of a case that I can see."

"Hang it all! It's as plain as a pikestaff! He's engaged to this woman–this Mrs. Truslove–who has a nice little income. He hears that her income is to be halved; and we know that if an allowance begins by being halved, as likely as not it will be stopped altogether before long. He saw that clearly enough. Then in the very nick of time this cheque comes along. He sends it to the bank with this letter of instructions, and murders Lord Loudwater so that he cannot disavow them. What more of a case do you want?"

"I don't want a better case. I only want some evidence. It's true enough that Mrs. Manley told me that she told Manley that Lord Loudwater proposed to halve her allowance. But where's the evidence that she talked to him about it? She'd deny it if you put her into the witness-box, and you can't put her into the witness-box."

"Husband and wife, by Jove! Oh, the clever young scoundrel!" cried Mr. Carrington.

"And that halving of the allowance is the beginning of the whole business. Manley had made up his mind to marry a lady with a fixed income—indeed, they were probably already engaged. Loudwater upsets the arrangement. Manley restores the *status quo* by means of this cheque and the murder of Loudwater. Of course, he hated Loudwater—he admitted as much to me—more than once. But if Loudwater had played fair about that allowance, he'd be alive now. Having established the *status quo*, Manley promptly marries the lady, and closes the mouth of the only person who can bear witness that the allowance was in danger and he had any motive for murdering Loudwater."

Mr. Carrington ground his teeth and murmured: "The infernal young scoundrel!" Then he broke out violently: "But we're not beaten yet. Now that we know for a fact that he murdered Loudwater and why, there must be some way of getting at him."

"I very much doubt it," said Flexen sadly. "He's an uncommonly able fellow. I don't believe that he's taken a chance. He wears a glove and leaves the knife in the wound, so that there are no bloodstains. And consider the cheque. The bank wouldn't have honoured Loudwater's own cheque, the cheque of a dead man, but the stock-broker's cheque goes through as a matter of course."

"Of course," said Mr. Carrington.

"And he has kept the business so entirely in his own hands. If we had run in anyone else, he'd have come forward and sworn that he heard Loudwater snore after Roper had seen that person leave the Castle. I'm beginning to think that he's one of the most able murderers I ever heard of. I certainly never came across one in my own experience who was a patch on him," said Mr. Flexen.

"Don't be in such a hurry to lose hope. There must be some way of getting at him—there must be," said Mr. Carrington obstinately.

"I'm glad to hear it," said Mr. Flexen in a tone of utter scepticism.

They walked on, Mr. Flexen reflecting on Mr. Manley's ability, Mr. Carrington cudgelling his brains for a method of bringing his crime home to him. At the door of his office Mr. Flexen held out his hand.

"Come along in. I've got an idea," said Mr. Carrington.

17

Mr. Flexen shrugged his shoulders with a sceptical air. He had not formed a high opinion of Mr. Carrington's intelligence. However, he followed him into his office and sat down, ready to give him his best attention.

Mr. Carrington wore a really hopeful expression, and he said: "My idea is that we should get at Manley through Mrs. Manley."

"I'm not at all keen on getting at a man through his wife," said Mr. Flexen rather dolefully. "But in this case it's manifestly our duty to leave nothing untried. Murder for money is murder for money."

"I should think it *was* our duty!" cried Mr. Carrington with emphasis.

"And there are three innocent people under suspicion of having committed the murder. Fire away. How is it to be done?" said Mr. Flexen.

"The new Lord Loudwater must bring an action against Mrs. Manley for the return of that twelve thousand pounds on the ground that it was obtained from the late Lord Loudwater by fraud—as it certainly was," said Mr. Carrington, leaning forward with shining eyes and speaking very distinctly.

"I see," said Mr. Flexen. But his expression was not hopeful.

"Once we get her in the witness-box we establish the fact that Lord Loudwater had made up his mind to halve her allowance, for she'll have to give the reason for her visiting him so late that night; and so we get Manley's motive for committing the murder also established."

"I see. But will you be able to use her evidence in the first trial at the second?" said Mr. Flexen doubtfully.

"That's the idea," said Mr. Carrington triumphantly.

"You think it can be worked?"

"We can have a jolly good try at it," said Mr. Carrington, rubbing his hands together, and his square, massive face was rather malignant in its triumph.

Mr. Flexen did not look triumphant, or even hopeful.

"But will you get the new Lord Loudwater to bring this action?" he said.

"Why, of course. There's the money for one thing, and when he sees how important it is from the point of view of getting at Manley, he can't refuse," said Mr. Carrington confidently.

"There isn't the money—not necessarily. He might get back the twelve thousand pounds and have to pay Mrs. Manley six hundred a year for forty or fifty years. She's a healthy-looking woman," said Mr. Flexen. "I take it that the late Lord Loudwater had property of his own against which she could claim."

"Oh, of course, she could do that," said Mr. Carrington, and there was some diminution of the triumphant expression.

"She would," said Mr. Flexen. "Then you'll have to get over his objection to incurring a considerable amount of odium. It will look bad for a man of his wealth to try to recover from a lady a sum of money to which everyone will consider her entitled."

"Oh, but it was obtained by fraud," said Mr. Carrington.

"If you were sure of proving that, it would make a difference in the way people would regard it. But you're not sure of proving it—not by a long chalk. And you can't assure your client that you are. There'll be a lot of conflicting evidence about that signature, as Harrison pretty clearly showed. If you don't prove it, your client will be landed with the costs of the case and incur still greater odium."

"Ah, but he is bound to take the risk to bring his cousin's murderer to justice," said Mr. Carrington.

"Is he?" said Flexen dryly. "What kind of terms was he on with his murdered cousin?"

"Well, I must say I didn't expect you to ask that question," said Mr. Carrington pettishly. "What kind of terms was the late Lord Loudwater likely to be on with his heir? They hated one another like poison."

"I thought as much," said Mr. Flexen. "And what kind of a man is the new man—anything like his dead cousin?"

"Oh, well, all the Loudwaters are pretty much of a muchness. But the present man is a better man all round—better manners and better brains," said Mr. Carrington.

"Better brains, and you think he'll be willing to celebrate his succession to the peerage by a first-class scandal of this kind, a scandal which may bring him this money, but which will certainly bring odium on him?" said Mr. Flexen.

"When it's a case of bringing a murderer to justice," said Mr. Carrington obstinately.

"The murderer of a man he hated like poison? I should think that he'd want to see his way pretty clear. And it isn't clear—not by any means. For there's precious little chance of Mrs. Manley's giving Lord Loudwater's threat to halve her allowance as the reason of her visit to him that night. In fact, there's no chance at all. Manley will see to that. Once attack the genuineness of that signature, and you open his eyes to his danger. She'll come into the witness-box with quite another reason for that visit, and a good reason too. Manley will find it for her," said Mr. Flexen with conviction. "But there's the quarrel. She can't get over that quarrel," said Mr. Carrington stubbornly.

"She'll deny the quarrel. It's only Mrs. Carruthers' word against hers. Besides, Mrs. Carruthers heard what she did hear through a closed door. It will be so easy to make out that she made a mistake."

"You seem to take it for granted that Mrs. Manley will commit perjury at that young scoundrel's bidding," snapped Mr. Carrington.

"I take it for granted that she'll be a woman fighting to save her husband. And I'm also sure that there'll be precious few mistakes in tactics made in the fight. I think that all you'll get out of the trial will be a strong presumption that Lord Loudwater committed suicide. I'd bet that that is the line Manley will take. And she'll make a thundering good witness for him. She's a good-looking woman, with plenty of intelligence."

Mr. Carrington gazed at him with unhappy eyes. His square, massive face had lost utterly its expression of triumph.

"But hang it all!" he cried. "What are we going to do? Knowing what we know, we can't sit still and do nothing."

"I can't see *anything* we can do," said Mr. Flexen frankly, and he rose. "You have demonstrated that Manley's position is impregnable."

He took his leave of the dejected lawyer.

Outside Mr. Carrington's office he stood still, hesitating. He could have caught a train back to Low Wycombe, but he could not bring himself to take it. He could not at once tear himself away from London and Mr. Manley. He must sleep on the new facts in the Loudwater case. He went to his club, engaged a bedroom, and dined there.

Mr. and Mrs. Manley dined at their flat. Mr. Manley talked during dinner with elegance and vivacity. The maid brought in the coffee and went back to the kitchen.

As he lighted his wife's cigarette, Mr. Manley said in a careless tone: "What did Flexen want to see you about?"

Helena gave him a full account of her interview with Mr. Flexen, his questions and her answers.

"I guessed that you were the *Daily Wire's* mysterious woman," he said. "I saw how frightened you were when it came out. But, of course, as you didn't say anything about it, I didn't."

"That is so like you," she murmured. "One human being should never intrude on another," said Mr. Manley with a noble air.

"It might be your motto," she said, looking at him with admiring eyes. She paused; then she added: "And I was frightened–horribly frightened. I couldn't sleep. I was going to tell you about it, but I didn't like to. You gave me no opening. Then the letter came from my bankers–about the twelve thousand pounds–and it made it all right. It made it clear that I had no reason to murder Loudwater."

"Of course," said Mr. Manley. "But in the event of any new developments, I should not admit that Lord Loudwater talked of halving your allowance, or that you quarrelled with him. In fact, I shouldn't let Flexen interview you again at all. In an affair of this kind you can't be too careful."

"I won't let him interview me again," said Helena with decision.

Mr. Flexen did not try to interview her again. But at eleven the next morning he called on Mr. Manley. He had very little hope of effecting anything by the call, though he meant to try. But he had the keenest desire to scrutinize him again and carefully in the light of the new facts he had discovered.

Mr. Manley kept him waiting awhile in the drawing-room; then the maid ushered him into Mr. Manley's study. Mr. Manley was sitting at a table, at work on his play. He greeted Mr. Flexen with a rather absent-minded air.

Mr. Flexen surveyed him with very intent, measuring eyes. At once he perceived that he had rather missed Mr. Manley's jaw in giving attention to his admirable forehead. It was, indeed, the jaw of a brute. He could see him drive the knife into Lord Loudwater, and walk out of the smoking-room with an ugly, contented smile on his face.

He had little hopes of bringing off anything in the nature of a bluff; but he said, in a rasping tone: "We've discovered that the signature of Lord Loudwater's letter of instructions to his bankers to pay that cheque for twelve thousand pounds into your wife's account was forged."

Mr. Manley looked at him blankly for a moment. There was no expression at all on his face. Then it filled slowly with an expression of surprise.

"Rehearsed, by Jove!" murmured Mr. Flexen under his breath, and he could not help admiring the skilful management of that expression of surprise. It was so unhasty and natural.

"My dear fellow, what on earth are you driving at? I saw him write it myself," said Mr. Manley in an indulgent tone.

"You forged it," snapped Mr. Flexen.

Mr. Manley looked at him with a new surprise which changed slowly to pity. Then he said in such a tone as one might use to an unreasonable child: "My good chap, what on earth should I forge it *for*?"

"You knew that he was going to halve Mrs. Truslove's allowance. You were bent on marrying a woman with money. You took this way of ensuring that she had money, forged the letter, and murdered Lord Loudwater," said Mr. Flexen on a rising inflexion.

"By Jove! I see what you're after. It shows how infernally silly a schoolboy joke can be! Lord Loudwater never talked of halving my wife's allowance. That was an invention of mine. I told her that he was doing so just to tease her," said Mr. Manley firmly, with a note of contrition in his voice.

Mr. Flexen opened his mouth a little way. It was a superb invention. It left Mrs. Manley free to go into the witness-box to tell the story she had told him. It knocked the bottom clean out of Carrington's case.

"What really happened was that Lord Loudwater was grousing about the allowance—at being reminded every six months that he had behaved like a cad. I suggested that he should pay her a lump sum and be done with the business. He jumped at the idea. The cheque had come from his stockbrokers that morning; he directed me to write that letter of instructions to his bankers; I wrote it, and he signed it. There you have the whole business."

"I don't believe a word of it!" cried Mr. Flexen.

Mr. Manley rose with an air of great dignity and said: "My good chap, I can excuse your temper. It was an ingenious theory, and it must be very annoying to have it upset. But I'm fed up with this Loudwater business. I've got here"–he tapped the manuscript on the table–"a drama worth fifty of it. Out of working hours I don't mind talking that affair over with you; in them I won't."

Mr. Flexen rose and said: "You're undoubtedly the most accomplished scoundrel I've ever come across."

"If you will have it so," said Mr. Manley patiently. Then he smiled and added: "Praise from an expert–"

They turned to see Mrs. Manley standing in the doorway, her lips parted, her eyes dilated in a growing consternation.

She stepped forward. Mr. Flexen slipped round her and fairly fled.

She looked at Mr. Manley with horror-stricken eyes and said: "What–what did he mean, Herbert?"

"He meant what he said. But what it really means is that I won't let him hang that wretched James Hutchings," said Mr. Manley with a noble air.

*   *   *   *   *

Three months later, on the first night of Mr. Manley's play, Colonel Grey came upon Mr. Flexen in the lounge of the Haymarket, between the second and third acts. Both of them praised the play warmly, and there came a pause.

Then Colonel Grey said: "I suppose you've given up all hope of solving the problem of Loudwater's death."

"Oh, I solved it three months ago. It was Manley," said Mr. Flexen.

"By Jove!" said Colonel Grey softly.

"Not a doubt of it. I'll tell you all about it one of these days," said Mr. Flexen, for the bell rang to warn them that the third act was about to begin.

In the corridor Colonel Grey said: "Queer that he should have dropped down dead in the street a week before this success."

"Well, he was discharged from the Army for having a bad heart. But it is a bit queer," said Mr. Flexen.

"The mills of God," said Colonel Grey.

"Looks like it," said Mr. Flexen.

THE END

Resurrected Press Mysteries from the Dr. John Thorndyke Series

Dr. John Thorndyke - Lecturer on Medical Jurisprudence and Forensic Medicine. Before Bones, before CSI, before Quincy, M.E – there was Dr. John Thorndyke solving the most baffling cases of Edwardian London using the latest tools of medical science. Read about his cases in:

The Eye of Osiris
John Bellingham, noted Egyptologist has vanished not once but twice in the same day. Now Dr, Thorndyke must unravel the tangled claims on his estate, solve the riddle of the missing man and find the "Eye of Osiris".

The Mystery of 31 New Inn
When Dr. Jervis is whisked away in a coach with no windows to an unknown location to treat a man in a coma from undivulged causes it is Dr. Thorndyke who must come up with the solution.

The Red Thumb Mark
The first of Dr. Thorndyke's cases finds him trying to prove the innocence of a young man accused of being a diamond thief despite the fact that his finger print was found at the scene of the crime.

John Thorndyke's Cases
More cases of medical mysteries as told by his trusted assistant Jervis, M.D. Eight stories of crime and deduction in Edwardian London.

Visit www.resurrectedpress.com

Resurrected Press Mysteries by John R. Watson & Arthur J. Rees

The Hampstead Mystery

High Court Justice Sir Horace Fewbanks found shot dead in his Hampstead home, a butler with a criminal past, a scorned lover and a hint of scandal. These are the elements of the Hampstead Mystery that Detective Inspector Chippenfield of Scotland Yard must unravel with the assistance of the ambitious Detective Rolfe. But will he be able to sort out the tangled threads of this case and arrest the culprit before he is upstaged by the celebrated gentleman detective Crewe. Follow the details of this amazing case at it plays out across Hampstead, London and Scotland until it reaches a stunning conclusion in the courts of the Old Bailey.

The Mystery of the Downs

When Harry Marsland was caught in a sudden down pour he sought shelter at Cliff Farm. Met at the door by a young woman clearly expecting someone else he is only too glad to get inside to wait out the storm. When they hear a noise upstairs in the deserted house they investigate only to discover the body of the farm's owner, Frank Lumsden, dead of a gunshot wound. Who then, killed Lumsden, and why? Who was the woman expecting and did she have any roll in the murder? These are the questions that private detective Crewe must answer in The Mystery of the Downs.

Visit www.resurrectedpress.com

Other Resurrected Press Mysteries

Mysteries on a Train

Before the Orient Express there was:

The Rome Express by Arthur Griffiths

A man is found dead in his first class sleeping compartment on the express from Rome to Paris. Who was his murderer? The Countess? The English General? His brother the clergy man? The maid who has disappeared? Is the French justice system up to solving the crime? Read about it in The Rome Express.

The Passenger from Calais by Arthur Griffiths

Colonel Basil Annesley finds he is the only passenger on the train from Calais to Lucerne. That is until a mysterious woman shows up at the last minute to book a compartment. Who is after her? What is her secret? Is she a criminal or a victim? Read about it in The Passenger from Calais

Visit us at www.resurrectedpress.com

Resurrected Press Mysteries by J. S. Fletcher

The Orange-Yellow Diamond

When an elderly pawnbroker is murdered in the London parish of Paddington, a young, down on his luck writer is accused of the crime. But then it's found the pawnbroker had had in his possession an extraordinary South African diamond worth over eighty-thousand pounds — a diamond that's now missing. It falls to Melky Rubenstein to unravel the mystery and prove the young man's innocence.

The Middle Temple Murder

When an elderly man's body is found on the steps of chambers in the Midde Temple, one of the Inns of Court, it falls to newspaperman Frank Spargo and Detective-Sergeant Rathbury to solve the crime. The murdered man, for indeed it was murder, was found with no money or identification on his person except for a piece of paper with the name and address of a young barrister. Who is the victim? Why was he killed? Who is the murderer?

Scarhaven Keep

Bassett Oliver, the famed actor, has gone missing. When Oliver fails to show for a rehearsal, aspiring playwright Richard Copplestone finds himself sent to the small village of Scarhaven on the northern coast of England to track down the actors movements. What he finds is mystery. Find the answers as Copplestone unravels the mystery of Scarhaven Keep.

Visit www.resurrectedpress.com

Resurrected Press Mysteries by Fergus Hume

The Green Mummy

Professor Braddock hoped to compare the burial practices of the Egyptians with those of the ancient Peruvians with his latest acquisition, the mummy of the last Inca, Caxas. But on arrival, the packing case proved to hold not the mummy, but the body of his assistant Sidney Bolton. It falls to Archie Hope to discover the murderer if he is to marry the professors step-daughter, Lucy Kendal. Who killed Bolton and where is the mummy? Was it the sea captain Hervey? The mysterious Don Pedro? Cockatoo the Polynesian servant? The professor, himself? And what has become of the emeralds? These are the questions that Hope must answer amongst the secrets of the past in The Green Mummy.

The Mystery of a Hansom Cab

"Truth is said to be stranger than fiction, and certainly the extraordinary murder which took place in Melbourne Friday morning goes a long way towards verifying that saying." Thus opens The Mystery of a Hansom Cab, the best selling mystery of the nineteenth century. When a man is found dead in a hansom cab one of Melbourne's leading citizens is accused of the murder. He pleads his innocence, yet refuses to give an alibi. It falls to a determined lawyer and an intrepid detective to find the truth, revealing long kept secrets along the way. Fergus Hume's first and perhaps most famous mystery... The Mystery Of A Hansom Cab.

Visit www.resurrectedpress.com

Resurrected Press Mysteries From Louis Tracy

The Albert Gate Mystery
Four men murdered and a fortune in diamonds belonging to the Turkish Sultan stolen, while the Foreign Office official in charge has gone missing. Was it a common jewelry theft or was it a case of international intrigue? This is the question that barrister detective Reginald Brett must solve.

The Bartlett Mystery
When Ronald Tower is murdered on his way to a bridge game on the yacht Sans Souci it at first appears a common crime. But as Rex Carshaw finds, a tragic case of mistaken identity leads to political scandal among the rich and powerful of New York.

The Strange Case of Mortimer Fenley
When the wealthy Mortimer Fenley is struck down by a shot from an express rifle on the steps of his mansion, detectives Winter and Furneaux of Scotland Yard must find the culprit. Was it the artist who claimed he was painting a picture at the time of the shot? The disaffected younger son? Or is there another suspect?

The Stowmarket Mystery
For five generations the Fergus-Hume family has been cursed. Each of the baronets has met a violent end. When the fifth baronet is found slain by a ceremonial Japanese dagger, suspicion falls on his cousin David. It falls to barrister detective Reginald Brett to prove his innocence and find the real murder in a case that spans two continents and as many centuries.

Visit www.resurrectedpress.com

About Resurrected Press

A division of Intrepid Ink, LLC, Resurrected Press is dedicated to bringing high quality, vintage books back into publication. See our entire catalogue and find out more at www.ResurrectedPress.com.

About Intrepid Ink, LLC

Intrepid Ink, LLC provides full publishing services to authors of fiction and non-fiction books, eBooks and websites. From editing to formatting, from publishing to marketing, Intrepid Ink gets your creative works into the hands of the people who want to read them. Find out more at www.IntrepidInk.com.